TURN

Global Endeavor
PUBLISHING

ALSO BY PAUL B KOHLER

An Anthology of Short Stories
Winter 2016

The Hunted Assassin

The Borrowed Souls

The Immortality Chronicles
Rememorations (contributed)

Linear Shift, A Novel

Silo Sage: Recoil

An Anthology of Short Stories
Summer 2014

Something to Read: A Charity Anthology
Four Stories Contributed

TURN

BOOK ONE OF THE HUMANITY'S EDGE TRILOGY

Turn: Book One of the Humanity's Edge Trilogy is a work of fiction. Names, characters, places, and incidents either are the product of the author's imagination or are used fictitiously. Any resemblance to actual persons, living or dead, events, or locales is entirely coincidental.

Edited by Amy Maddox and Allison Krupp
Cover design by Paul B. Kohler
Interior design and layout by Paul B. Kohler

ISBN-13: 978-1-940740-17-1
ISBN-10: 1-940740-17-7

www.paulkohler.net

Give feedback on the book at:
Amazon: amazon.com/author/paulkohler
info@paul-kohler.net
Twitter: @PaulBKohler
Facebook: facebook.com/Paul.B.Kohler.Author

Printed in the United States of America

First Edition

For Alicia

Because you are the most wonderful daughter in the whole wide world.

1.

Darcy scrambled up the hayloft ladder, an entire kaleidoscope of butterflies fluttering deep inside her. She could feel the scratchy straw beneath her fingers as she gripped each rung, but she didn't mind. She was breathless, her knees quick to bend and snap back. Far below, she felt Caleb's eyes watching her ass, gauging the darkness beneath her skirt where her legs met. The moment she reached the top, she whirled around, her dark hair skimming over her eyes. She blinked haltingly.

"Are you coming up, or are you too scared?" she taunted, tilting an exposed shoulder toward him.

Caleb laughed, his broad, quarterback shoulders shaking slightly. A bit of eighteen-year-old five-o'clock shadow dusted his cheeks and upper lip. His eyes gleamed with lust for her.

"You sure you want to do this?" he asked her, raising a thick eyebrow high.

"Just come on, before my dad hears us," Darcy sighed. She beckoned, allowing him to see an inch of cleavage before ripping herself back toward the hay bales in the loft, listening as he climbed.

The pair had left the football game only thirty minutes before, speeding out across the dirt roads and toward her father's farm, ditching their friends and their typical pizza joint. This night was different.

It sizzled with something special.

When Caleb finally appeared in the hayloft, his face glinted in the moonlight, a slight gash beneath his right eye—a memento from the game. Darcy reached toward him, touching it delicately with her thumb. “Caleb, I didn’t think they hit you so hard,” she whispered, breathless. The moment she touched him, the tension between them broke, and he turned toward her, catching her lips with his.

She wrapped her arms around his shoulders, feeling the force of his upper arms and back muscles. She allowed herself to forget about her father, only a heartbeat away, reading in the farmhouse. She was a young woman, brimming with endless sexuality. In a moment she felt Caleb’s fingers attack her cardigan’s buttons, ripping the top ones apart.

She broke the kiss, looking at him with misty, doe eyes. “Oh, Caleb,” she whispered.

“What?” he asked. His lips were red from the passion of their kisses.

“It’s just—it’s different this time. It feels like—like maybe—” she shook her head, the single word tickling along her tongue. “It feels like maybe I’m in love with you.”

Caleb didn’t move. He held her tight, looking at her with reassuring eyes. “I love you, too,” he said. His voice was deep, carnal. Almost like a hero’s in an old movie.

As Darcy leaned in closer to him, to catch him in a kiss once more, she noted that his eyes suddenly looked out behind her, toward the field and the pine-covered hills beyond. His jaw dropped, and his arms swept around Darcy, almost in a tackle.

“Holy shit, Darcy. Look!” He pointed toward the open bay door in the loft, inhaling sharply.

Darcy frowned slightly before turning toward Caleb's extended arm. There, in the distance, was the most remarkable shooting star she'd ever seen. She slipped from Caleb's embrace, feeling her breasts strain against her partially unbuttoned cardigan. She felt Caleb appear beside her as they crept toward the open window, watching as the shooting star seemed to burn light upon the field.

"It looks like it's getting closer. But that's impossible," Darcy whispered, shaking her head. "It must be a million miles away."

But Caleb took a step back, grasping Darcy's hand. "Darcy. No. It's coming right for us," he said, his voice cracking.

Darcy stared into his eyes, the moment filled with tension and fear. She shot a fleeting glance back toward the shooting star, seeing that, sure enough, it was bearing toward them. It was now only about thirty feet above the trees that skirted around the field. It seemed like a bull's eye. Like it knew they were there, waiting.

"WE HAVE TO RUN!" Caleb shouted, shooting his arm around Darcy's small waist. "Come ON!"

But Darcy's mind was too far away. She suddenly felt outside of herself, floating in the stars above. She thought she could even feel the heat from the streaming orb, shining against her cheeks. "It's beautiful," she whispered, her pupils drowning out her pale blue eyes. "And besides," she said, as the star whizzed closer, "if we run away now, my dad will see us. He'll know we were about to—"

"IT DOESN'T MATTER. NOT IF WE DIE!" Caleb thrust her toward the ladder they'd only just climbed, launching her over the edge and toward a mammoth haystack below. As Darcy fell, her hair swept back.

She was flying, feeling the rush of the shooting star in her ears in the moments before she landed.

Immediately after Caleb threw Darcy from the loft, he turned briefly, curiosity running through him. Just as he spun, the meteorite made its final plunge toward the barn and crashed directly into the hayloft. It struck Caleb's chest—dead center—blasting him through the air and to the ground, nearly fifteen feet below.

He died instantly.

Far below the wreckage in the hayloft, Darcy lay still. Smoke filtered from the barn. The sky was dark, without stars. And the meteorite steamed in the dirt.

2.

Sheriff Clay Dobbs slipped socks over his feet, leaning heavily over the side of the bed. Fatigue made his arms weak, and they hung lazily as he blinked at the clock on the nightstand. It was already past eight in the morning, after a night of monitoring the football game for the high school. Throughout the evening he'd thwarted a small incident of vandalism, run several testosterone-filled teen boys back to their cars, and then, ultimately, collapsed on a chair in his living room upon his release. It wasn't a heavy load for a sheriff, sure. But it was a small town. And keeping watch over the tiny comings and goings of the high school was a pleasure for him, especially given that his only daughter, Maia, was a freshman.

Valerie, his wife of nineteen years and his girlfriend for many more than that, was cooking eggs and bacon in the kitchen. He rambled down the steps, finding Maia already seated, sipping orange juice.

"What, no coffee today?" he asked her, teasing. He drifted his fingers over her fine hair, noting that she hardly looked up from her book.

Clay stole a kiss from his wife before taking a seat and sipping from his own mug of brew, gazing at his daughter. She was becoming gorgeous, no longer the little girl who'd played in the mud and banged up her knees. He knew it was cliché to think like this. To say the words, "Man, it all happens so fast." But it truly did.

"Maia?" he said, his eyes coaxing. "Do you want to tell me what's up? It's a Saturday, and you're not sleeping in till three in the afternoon. I assume you must be sick or something."

Maia smirked, turning a page. "Maybe a little. Plus, I couldn't sleep," she said, swallowing with obvious pain.

Clay turned his eyes toward his wife, who shrugged her slight shoulders. She filled a plate with eggs and bacon and tucked it in front of Clay, the floor creaking slightly as she leaned. "We've both been awake for almost an hour. You, Sheriff Clay, are the sleepy one in this house."

"Well. I suppose I have both of you to thank for holding down the fort," he said, rubbing his hands together. The steam from breakfast crept over his face. "Why couldn't you sleep, pumpkin?"

"Ugh," Maia said, rolling her eyes. She snapped her book on the table and leaned heavily against her hands, casting her gaze out the window. "Something horrible happened at school yesterday. I don't want to talk about it."

Clay's heart cringed. He felt vaguely panicked, realizing that he didn't have much experience solving a teenage girl's problems. Sure, he had saved the town from that rampant robber the previous year, and any sign of spousal abuse—he was on it. But as far as his own daughter was concerned, he was out of his depths.

"Why don't you want to talk about it?" he asked her.

Maia pushed her cheeks out with air, widening

her eyes. "It was so embarrassing yesterday. I asked a boy to the dance."

The words hung in the air. Clay turned his eyes toward his wife, who had a single hand upon her hip. She beckoned toward her husband, as if to tell him to work harder, to say something. She was his coach.

"And it didn't go the way you planned?" Clay asked, his voice tentative.

"No, Dad. It didn't go exactly the way—"

Clay lifted his hands in the air, instantly realizing his mistake. He felt a wave of anger from his suddenly pubescent daughter. But as his expression changed, Maia turned her eyes back toward the table, shaking her head.

"I'm sorry, Dad. You know it's not like me to snap. I think I'm catching that flu running around school."

Clay sighed slightly, worried. "It's okay, pumpkin. We all have shit days sometimes. Load up on the vitamin C to start."

Maia barely looked up but held her half-drunk glass of orange juice up for all to see.

Valerie made a throat noise beside him. Although they were aligned on nearly every element of their parenting styles, she didn't always agree with the amount of cursing Clay did in front of their daughter. As a slight joke, Clay snuck his fingers over his lips, as if to "zip them." He tossed an invisible key to the floor. His daughter snickered, thus ensuring they were on the same side.

Clay breathed a sigh of relief.

But as he did, his cell phone buzzed on the table. It was the station. His face turned stony and serious. The station didn't ordinarily call him over the weekend unless something had gone wrong.

"Dobbs," he answered, his voice firm.

As he listened, his face turned green, then grey. Both his wife and daughter paused, their eyes concerned. As the other end seemed to drivel on, Valerie allowed the second batch of bacon to burn. Maia leaned forward attentively, seeming to have already forgotten about the "incident" at school altogether.

"Yes. I understand," Clay said curtly. "Any survivors?"

Valerie and Maia looked at each other then, shock splayed across their faces.

"And her condition?" he asked. His voice hung in the air, waiting. "Okay. I understand. I'll be on my way shortly," he affirmed. He dropped the phone back on the table and stood, rubbing his temples as he thought.

"What was that?" Valerie asked, still holding the spatula attentively.

"Well, it seems there was a fire early this morning out at the Crawford farm," he said. "Darcy's at the hospital. She's been in and out of consciousness."

Maia's eyes grew wide. She and Darcy Crawford were classmates and had known each other for practically their entire lives.

"They tell me that the barn's gone. Burned up. And there's one dead, not sure who yet," he said, opting to withhold Caleb's name until he was certain his parents had been notified. He bounded toward the door, stopping long enough to slip on his shoes. "That's all I know right now. I've got to head in to the station. I'll call later when I have more information."

Valerie and Maia followed him closely as he walked toward the door, both of them embracing him in a hug before he stepped outside. He felt his heart brim with love for them both, although the duty to his town forced him to walk quickly, away from this safety.

The world was a wretched place, he thought as he turned the key in the ignition. But being sheriff had certain responsibilities attached, and dealing with unforeseen tragedies was one of them. Thankfully, they were quite infrequent.

But accidents happened, he assured himself. And whatever happened out at the Crawford place was certain to be just that. Avoiding those meant you avoided fate.

3.

Sheriff Dobbs drove swiftly through town, to where the sheriff station stood at the corner of Baker Street and Fifteenth. The notable early twentieth-century architectural landmark was the glory of Carterville. Across the street and down a half block was Clay's favorite coffee shop, and remembering that he'd left his steaming pile of bacon and eggs untouched at home, his craving for donuts was overpowering. But this wasn't the time for it, he grumbled as he pulled into his parking spot.

He bounded from his cruiser and nudged the door closed, giving a small wave to a woman walking toward the nearby bank. She looked at him with knowing eyes and smiled. Being the sheriff in a town as small as Carterville, everyone knew everyone and what you were up to. Clay eased his hand over the back of his neck, breaking his eye contact. Although he could recognize most everyone by face, he couldn't quite remember this woman's name.

Inside the police station, Jean, his longtime dispatcher and receptionist, greeted him. She stood at her desk, holding a stack of crumpled messages. "Sheriff," she said firmly. "So sad to hear the news about Crawford farm."

"Yes, well," Clay said, shifting his weight. He rested a hand on his holster and tapped at it with an absent finger. "I suppose these things happen, unfortunately. What do you have there?" He gestured toward the handful of papers.

Jean thrust them forward. "The whole town is grieving about what happened to that poor boy. And about Darcy. God, that girl got lucky, didn't she? I can't even imagine."

Clay looked at the messages with relative disdain. He hadn't gotten into the business of saving lives and protecting towns to go through paperwork. But he nodded, knowing that they carried the weight of empathy from the town, a town he had grown to love since he'd settled there nearly fifteen years before. "I'll take care of them. Thanks, Jean. Is Alayna in yet?"

Jean's eyebrows shot high. "She's been here for almost a half hour. She's waiting for you in your office."

"Ah. She's going to scold me, isn't she?"

"I think you have some harsh words coming," Jean teased, winking.

Alayna was Clay's deputy, a thirty-something woman who'd grown up a local, leaving only briefly for school. She'd long joked that no matter how much she wanted to, she'd never find a better life outside of the town's limits. "They just don't get me out there, Clay," she'd said over and over, half joking.

Clay proceeded toward his office and popped the door open, revealing Alayna Cordell before him. She sat in his office chair, her boots idle upon his desk and her arms behind her head. She gave no indication of moving. As their eyes met, a smirk stretched across her face. "Hey there, boss."

"Alayna. Fancy finding you here, relaxing in *my* office," Clay said, latching the door closed behind him. "You know, if you want my job, my pay, and this desk to rest your feet on for the rest of time, all you have to do is return every one of the fifty or so messages Jean just handed me." He dropped the stack on his desk and tilted his head. "What do you say?"

Alayna dropped her boots to the floor and reached for the papers, sighing. "I suppose I can't lounge around here all day. You run such a tight ship." She gestured toward the empty coffee cup and the half-eaten donut beside her, Clay's remnants from the previous day.

Clay chuckled. Alayna was his second deputy, and a damn fine one. The one before, a man named Chris, had fled back to Dallas, where his father had arranged an accounting job, a nine-to-five, a position of safety. Chris hadn't had the grit to be a lawman.

Finally Alayna relinquished the seat, lending it back to its owner. "I was just waiting for you to roll your lazy bones in," she said, still reading over the grieving messages. "Man, this town really pulls all the stops for tragedies, doesn't it?"

"It's a compassionate community, that's for sure," Clay agreed, easing into his chair. "So. Since you've been here, I take it you've read through some of the report?"

"Yep," Alayna said, eyeing him. The light had gone out from her eyes. "The barn's completely gone. And you probably know that Darcy Crawford's in the hospital. The boy, Caleb, he didn't make it. I think the coroner's planning to take him, but I don't yet have word if he's still out at the farm."

"Thank you," Clay said, rubbing his fingers absently against his chin. "And nobody's set eyes on the barn yet?"

"Nope. I mean, none of the other deputies have gone out yet," she said. "I was thinking we could go."

Clay nodded. "One of us to the barn. The other to visit Darcy in the hospital. To pay our respects, and also to get some information about what happened. What do you think they were doing out in the barn so late at night, anyway?"

Alayna laughed lightly, shrugging. "What else do teenagers do in dark barns at night?"

Clay sighed. "I suppose you're right. Well. Shall we arm wrestle for the tasks? I certainly have no preference, and I'm still hanging on to my five-day winning streak."

Alayna rolled her eyes. She smacked her elbow upon the desk, nearly knocking the half-eaten donut to the ground. "All right. If I win, I'll take the hospital visit. I guess. I mean, in this case, I'm not sure who's the 'winner.'"

"Me neither," Clay sighed. But he snapped his hand upon Alayna's. They counted to three. Clay heard Alayna's grunts as she focused, trying to beam his hand back across the table. And as she strained, Clay felt himself release slightly, his mind falling toward fear of what they might find at the barn.

What if Caleb's body was still there, burned to a crisp?

He felt himself give up on the arm wrestling, then, knowing it was better for Alayna to meet with Darcy. He felt the cold table beneath his skin upon release. Alayna cheered, clapping her hands together, her eyes bright.

"Your winning streak, sir, is quite over," she said, laughing. "So I don't want to hear another brag out of you. Not for at least a week."

"I'm coming for you tomorrow," Clay said,

snapping his sheriff's hat over his head. "But in the meantime, I'll head out to the farm. The sooner you get up to visit Darcy, the better. The memory's fresh right now."

"Right," Alayna said, bringing her lips together in a grim line. "Good luck out there."

Clay felt the weight of the coming day upon his shoulders. He stood in the doorway, feeling the sunlight upon his cheeks, imagining, briefly, what it would be like to have his own daughter, Maia, in the hospital. Darcy's father, Mack—a widower who had raised Darcy on his own since his wife had died in the car accident several years before—was probably an absolute wreck.

4.

As Clay strode from his office, his mind revving, Jean held up her hand. He halted, peering toward her. She was on the phone, nodding.

"That's right. Okay. I'll let him know immediately." She dropped the receiver back in its cradle and turned toward him. She swallowed. "Apparently the mayor would like to speak with you before you begin this investigation."

Clay frowned, tilting his head. "Lois? That's who was on the phone?"

"She called herself. Personally," Jean nodded. A flicker of puzzlement swept across her eyes. "She's over at the Sunrise Diner. She says you can meet her there before you head out."

Perplexed, Clay bowed his head, thanking Jean, and then walked from the station. As he climbed into his cruiser, he tried to bolster his mindset. Just because the mayor wanted to speak with him now, before even getting started, didn't mean a thing. It was going to be just like any other investigation. Chances were, she just wanted to convey her sympathies about the death of the Latimer boy. She probably just wanted to ensure that everything was going to be handled with the utmost care. After all, nobody cared about Carterville more than Lois Washington. She'd been the mayor since before Clay had arrived in the town, and she ran an efficient township, ensuring that its people were safe, attending the silly town parties and parades, and not only kissing all the babies in a political move but also occasionally babysitting for them, as well.

Clay forged through town, flexing his fingers around the steering wheel anxiously. The Saturday morning traffic was vibrant, bustling. As he drove, several cars slowed their speed, shooting their foot to the brake pedal and giving him a hearty wave.

Clay stopped at the diner, which was only a mile and a half from the Crawford farm, and parked beside Lois's notable bright red car. As he entered, everyone inside turned their eyes toward him, chewing their food like a cow does its cud. He held up a hand in greeting and leaned toward the counter, where he whispered to the diner's owner. "Just a coffee, Theo, thanks."

Lois was seated in her usual booth beside the corner window. Her slight frame was a shadow in the sunlight, outlining her sharp nose and her high bun. The woman had never married and very much had the air of someone who didn't wish to share her life with anyone. She was a private person, but bright and warm. And the moment she saw Clay, she stood, shot her hand out to shake his, and gave him a sad, steady smile.

"What an event to wake up to," she said. "Darcy in the hospital, and poor Caleb." She shook her head, reseating herself before her breakfast of pancakes and bacon. Clay couldn't imagine how she kept such a trim figure.

"It's a tragic thing, Lois," Clay said, accepting his coffee from Theo. The warmth of the mug was pleasing upon his fingers. "I haven't even made it out to the farm yet, so I'm not sure how much I can say right now that you probably haven't already heard."

"Tell me what you do know," Lois said. She eyed him with an eagle's glare. It seemed the air had shifted around them.

"We know the barn caught fire somehow. The girl was protected from it, and her boyfriend, Caleb, perished in the blaze. According to Jean's report, Darcy's father, Mack, called it in and probably saved her life. I'm assuming Mack's at the hospital with her now, and Alayna's on her way to speak with them." Clay spoke in a rush, feeling the mayor's steely eyes upon him.

Lois nodded, slurping her orange juice. "All right. That all sounds fine," she said as she returned the glass back to the table. "Now listen here. I'd like to make a request through all of this."

"All of this?" Clay asked. "This accident?"

Lois's eyebrows rose high up on her forehead. "Sure. This accident. I'd like for you to exercise your best judgement throughout your investigation. You're a capable leader in this community, but we can't have things run off the rails here. In such a high-profile incident, there's certain to be . . . outside eyes and ears in our small community. Keep it low-key if possible, and keep me apprised of everything—and I mean everything. Do you understand?"

Clay leaned back heavily, feeling the plastic of the booth seat rub against his shirt. He'd never received such a brash request from the mayor, and it made his heart feel squeezed. Did she think he ordinarily made things too dramatic? Did she believe he often messed things up? Since he'd taken on the sheriff's position, there hadn't been a single scandal.

But he had no option but to agree. "Sure, Lois.

I'll keep things . . . under control. And I'll keep you in the loop, if you like," he said. He eyed his coffee, realizing he was wasting time. He needed to get out to the Crawfords'. "Now, if you don't mind, I have a tragedy to . . . suppress. You have some pancakes to focus on, anyway."

A false smile stretched across Lois's face. She looked sure, unemotional. "Sure, Clay. I know I can trust you." She shook his hand again and turned her neck toward him as he left. "Thanks for keeping our town safe, Sheriff," she called.

Strangely, Lois's words chilled Clay far more than they should have. He hurried from the diner, his eyes wide. And he sped from the parking lot, still shaking slightly, unsure of why Lois would tell him all this.

But the woman was growing older, he reasoned. And the only thing in the world she really cared about was the town. If she felt she needed to speak with him—even if it seemed like the silliest thing in the world—then, he supposed, he had to go along with it. It was just another quirk in a small town.

5.

Despite the fire that had burned all around her, Darcy wasn't in intensive care, or the burn unit, for that matter. Rather, the nurse told Alayna that Darcy had only a few bumps and bruises and was most likely suffering from a moderate concussion. "She's been in and out of consciousness, but she looks like she'll be okay," the nurse said, her eyes wide. "But the boy. What a tragedy this all is. And right before he could have played college football. All that potential."

Alayna wasn't sure what to say. She nodded awkwardly, her tongue frozen to the roof of her mouth, until the nurse spun toward the bright hallway. Alayna followed the nurse's squeaking tennis shoes, her police hat in her hands. A tight bun at the base of her neck, holding her black hair, stretched her skin, causing a minor headache.

The nurse led her to Darcy's room, where she lay silently, her arms folded over her chest and a white blanket tugged close to her neck. Her face was grim, scratched. Her teeth were clattering with cold, despite the air being a humid 75 degrees. Alayna frowned, sensing that the girl was in shock.

"Darcy," Alayna said, her voice soft. She eased into a chair beside the hospital bed. "Darcy, can you hear me?"

Darcy's eyes were wide open, searching the ceiling. She nodded blankly. "I'm sorry. I'm just so cold," she whispered.

"It's okay, Darcy. I know you must be going through a lot," Alayna said. She eased her hand over her arm. She wondered where Darcy's father was. Mack Crawford was a fine man, one she'd dealt with a few different times. And without the necessary "mothering" element of her personality, Alayna felt lost speaking with this teenage girl.

"It's cold, and then hot. W-what's wrong with me?" Darcy whispered. She eased her fingers over her forehead, flipping sweat from her pores. "Do you think we were just being punished?"

Alayna frowned. "For what? Punished for what?" she asked, shaking her head in confusion.

In that moment, Darcy's father entered the room, holding a bouquet of flowers. His eyes locked onto his daughter for a long moment. He held the flowers like a sword, then tapped them against his pectoral. He looked empty, defeated.

"Mack," Alayna said, standing from the plastic chair. She shook his hand. "Wanted to come down from the station to check on Darcy's condition."

Mack nodded curtly. "I appreciate that. We both do. She's—she's not feeling so good."

"I suppose I wouldn't be, either," Alayna affirmed. She kept steady eye contact with Mack, noting the discoloration in his cheeks. A bit of sweat ebbed on his forehead. He was shaking as well. If Alayna didn't know any better, she'd think they both had that damn flu bug. But surely it was just panic, altering their state of mind and body.

Mack dropped the bouquet of flowers into a glass vase and grasped his daughter's hand, eyeing Alayna once more from the other side of the bed. "It's strange, growing older. Knowing your entire happiness depends on the well-being of another. Of course, with your mother being the way she was, and your father being gone all those years—" he paused. Alayna felt slapped. "It must have been difficult for you, raising yourself like that."

Alayna took several deep, staggering breaths. She blinked several times before righting herself, giving him a brief smile. She knew he didn't mean it. News of her mother's alcoholism and father's abandonment had surely spread through the town like wildfire. Just because she'd put many years between her and those events didn't mean people didn't link her to them still. They were a part of her. And she was a part of the town.

"Anyway," Alayna said, attempting to change the subject, "they said she'll be okay?"

Mack nodded. Another bead of sweat dripped down his face. "We'll have to find someplace else to go when they release her," he told her. "The farmhouse was completely destroyed. The fire took both buildings. I managed to escape, but just barely."

Alayna jotted this information down on a pad, making the note: "Shivering. Both have flu—shock, or just panic?" beside it. "That must have been horrible for you," she said, her voice light. "Sheriff Dobbs has gone out to the farm now. He'll have answers to us soon. And in the meantime, you and Darcy should relax as best you can. Confusing times can make us ill in more ways than one." She passed her eyes over the father and daughter, feeling suddenly anxious.

After several minutes, Alayna excused herself and walked outside to the bright, near-autumn sunlight. She thought of Darcy, whose life had taken a dramatic turn in the previous several hours. When Alayna had been a teenager, cooking her own meals, shopping for groceries, trying to coax her mother to work in the days before she was officially fired, she hadn't felt that life could be bright, that hope would ever meet her somewhere down the line. She'd felt only darkness.

She trudged back toward her deputy vehicle, hoping she'd hear from Clay soon. She needed the kind of hope he brought to an investigation. She needed his insight.

6.

Clay Dobbs saw the smoke from only a half mile away as he sped down the country road. He frowned, feeling suddenly choked. They hadn't had such a dramatic death in the town in several years. Sure, there was the occasional car accident, the rare suicide. But this—a fire that overtook the very farm that most restaurants and grocers in town relied upon for dairy and meat—was something different. It felt intimate. Was it arson?

He parked far from the now-smoldering fire and marched toward it, his hands upon his hips. As he passed the field, he saw a fleck of fabric and heard footfalls before finding two farmhands before him. They peered toward him with frightened eyes. Their hands were restless.

"Sheriff, you're here!" one of them called. "We hoped someone would come out. The fire crew showed up and left, claiming the farm was a lost cause. Something about no water source near. We've only been here for an hour, and Mack is nowhere to be found, and this . . . disaster—"

Clay raised his hands, stretching his fingers high. "I'm here now. I'll check it out. Mack's at the hospital with Darcy." He eyed them curiously, noting that both were sweating profusely. The one who hadn't spoken was dabbing his forehead with a rag, mopping up sweat. They were also shivering, their teeth clattering. "Are you boys nervous about something, or are you coming down with that damn bug making its way around town?" he asked.

The pair made brief eye contact. "Maybe we should just go home," one stammered. "We'll get ahold of Mack and see what's up." He eyed the wreckage, the dark smoke. "I don't really want to go over there again. It seems . . . wrong somehow." Silence stretched long in the air.

As the farmhands crept back toward their trucks, Clay edged forward, his hand upon his gun. The farmhouse, a once glorious representation from the nineteenth century, was burned almost totally to the ground, leaving only a slight skeleton of the downstairs and a lonely stone chimney. The barn was completely obliterated, although Clay marched past red shards of barn wood as he grew closer. This made him feel that perhaps the barn had exploded, sending these wooden flecks so far from the source. But who would blow up a barn, so far out in the field?

Once he was close enough, he felt the heat. It was impenetrable, blasting against his cheeks and his forehead. He swiped his own rag from his pocket and blocked it over his cheeks and mouth, blinking wildly. He felt his eyebrows could singe off, that his eyes could melt into pools.

The barn was a dark, simmering mass of rubble, constantly eating at the remaining pieces of wood. Clay found a slight path through the devastation, thankful for his high-top boots, and stepped carefully around the glowing embers.

In the center of the once-barn structure, a crater had pushed deep into the earth. Clay edged toward it, feeling that this, perhaps, supported the bomb theory even more. As he drew closer, he felt he could hardly breathe. His lungs felt singed with the heat of the black smoke.

The moment he reached the crater, he tilted his head and peered into the darkness. The crater held a massive, glowing black rock that reflected the high sun, even through the smoke. It was clear that the rock was the cause of the fire . . . and all the surrounding destruction. And as Clay assessed it, his mouth open, confusion palpitating through him, his mind arrived at one very serious conclusion: a meteorite.

After several moments of gazing at the alien form, Clay backed away and spun from the black smoke, coughing. He leaned heavily, his hands upon his knees, choking and waiting for oxygen to come. Around him, the fields were empty. The sky was far too blue. Something was off. He felt far too alone.

Sheriff Dobbs returned to his cruiser, his mind stirring with the image of the meteorite, and pondered his options. Should he phone it in to the local university for study? Should he call the coroner and explain that he was unable to find a single sign of Caleb's body? Should he first call his deputy and marvel at the terrible nature of the earth and outer space, and at how nothing could have prevented this? Nothing at all?

He turned the ignition and began to drive back, still feeling the heat upon his cheeks. He sniffed, imagining the massive meteorite bearing down upon him—making it the very last thing he saw on earth. He knew this had been the reality for Caleb. Fear had given way to nothingness.

But once closer to town, Clay began to relax. He surveyed the passing cars and town inhabitants, carrying on with their days as if nothing was out of place. It was just another day in the life of Carterville.

He stopped at the only drive-thru restaurant in town and bought a small fry, reminding himself that he hadn't yet eaten, and that the salt—albeit unhealthy—would boost his blood flow. And besides, he wouldn't have to tell Valerie. Although surely she would smell it on him. That woman was sharp as a tack.

He drove easily into his normal spot at the station, leaned his head back, and shoveled ketchup-covered fries into his mouth, one after another. In this world of chance, he figured he might as well eat the whole damn thing.

7.

Clay stuffed the fast food bag into the side compartment as he crept from his cruiser. As he did so, Alayna pulled in beside him, giving him a quick wave and smile.

She met him at the front door, sighed intensely, and eyed him. “You look like you’ve just spent three days out in the sun,” she said.

Clay’s eyebrows went high. He touched his cheek, feeling its heat. “Well, that’s because I discovered much more than just a fire out at the Crawfords’,” he said. He leaned closer to her, his eyes dancing. “A meteorite.”

“What the hell?” she blurted. “Like, from outer space? Aliens and all that?”

Clay shook his head. He stomped his boot against the step, knocking farmhouse debris onto the concrete. “I mean, I wouldn’t go that far. But meteorites do exist, scientifically speaking. And sometimes they fall to earth—apparently choosing random lives to ruin at the same time.”

“Wow. That’s a bad day when a meteorite chooses you,” Alayna said, a bit flustered. She swallowed sharply. “I saw Darcy. And her father.”

“Is she doing all right?” Clay asked. With the scene from the farmhouse fresh in his mind, he couldn’t imagine how she could be. Everything had been scorched black. Any hay bales that had protected her had crisped out hours before.

"They said they're going to monitor her for a while yet, but they think she'll be okay," Alayna said, shrugging. "But she doesn't seem all right, mentally. She said what happened, and how Caleb was killed instantly. And Mack. First he lost his wife a few years ago, and now this? I think he might need a psych evaluation before this is over."

"I'm sure the docs will come to that same conclusion," Clay said uneasily. He gripped the station door, opening it for Alayna. They entered, smelling burnt coffee and stale donuts. The cliché was assuring.

As they moved through the entry, they noted that one of their deputies, Kyle, was releasing Trudy Benson from jail. Trudy was leaning heavily against the desk, watching with flirtatious eyes as Kyle signed her release form. She was sloppy, her blonde hair frizzy and wayward from sleeping in the jail cell once more. Black mascara streaked down her cheeks, giving her a clownish look. And the moment she saw Clay and Alayna, she all but squealed with happiness. As she traipsed toward them, Clay noted that she was sweating. She looked erratic, but that wasn't uncommon.

"Clay. Alayna," she said, her smile stretching wide. "I want to apologize, again, for . . . landing myself back in here." She shot her thumb toward the jail cell. "Another faceless night, one more terrible mistake. I didn't mean to. I—I never do."

Clay felt assured, if only for a moment, at the normality of this event. He stepped up to Kyle and read the report. It was quite typical. "Trudy was blackout, disorderly, and kissing people at the bar without their agreement. She was kicked out of two bars before being picked up near the station and taken into custody."

"You brought her in, Kyle?" Clay asked.

"And she tried to kiss me, too," Kyle affirmed, shaking his head. "What a goddamn mess."

Trudy giggled uncertainly, eyeing the three officers. "So. Is it okay if I leave, or—" She turned toward the door. The smell of her was horrid, a mix of body odor and whisky. Clay saw Alayna turn up her nose. He knew this was probably a memory for her. Her mother had been a terrible drunk before her death.

"Trudy, Trudy. We've been over this," Clay said. "You can't just run around, drunkenly kissing whoever you run across." He tilted his head, giving his voice a fatherly tone. "It's an invasion of privacy, and it could be termed sexual harassment."

"I know . . ." Trudy said, trailing off. She dropped her head and pouted her red lips like a child.

"Trudy, this is your seventh time here in just the last three years," Clay continued. "Seven times! It's like you've lost any semblance of self-control. Maybe you're sexually harassing us?" Clay said. "But we don't want you here anymore. You need to restrain yourself. Stop living this way. Let's not make this a habit . . . again."

Trudy batted her eyelashes. Clay knew she was the town temptress, generally getting her way when she used her body, her smile, her eyes—with the promise of pleasing men. As far as he knew, she hardly paid for any of her drinks. In exchange, she was flirtatious, happy to see anyone and everyone who entered the bars, and usually only went home to her slight studio apartment within town limits when the bars closed. She filled the role nicely. And yet he couldn't help but feel sorry for her. Trudy had been an intelligent girl in school. She'd been engaged, even, before breaking it off and heading to the big city for about a year. When she'd returned, she'd found her ex-boyfriend had married someone else. And that she'd latched on to the party lifestyle that she couldn't abandon. And people like Kyle, a sheriff's deputy, had to clean up her messes.

Trudy nodded in agreement. Then she shuffled toward the door, waving at them with fluttering fingers, and began her traditional route home. She didn't drive anywhere. She was drunk far too often to keep a driver's license.

Kyle rolled his eyes and sighed evenly. "She was up all night talking to me in there," he said, gesturing to the jail cell. "I didn't think she'd ever shut up. Does that woman get any sleep?"

"You know she keeps different hours than the rest of us," Clay said, slapping his hand upon his deputy's back. "Thank you for your work. You're keeping this place safe. Or at least a little less chaotic."

Clay and Alayna continued their path through the front office, where they separated. Alayna headed toward the vending machine and then to her office to fill out paperwork, and Clay retreated to his own office. It was only just after noon, and already the day had been incredibly, even terribly, eventful.

8.

Back in his office, Clay rested his feet on the edge of the desk, tapping his pen upon the surface. He cradled the phone between his cheek and shoulder, dialing the unfamiliar number and noting that despite having only eaten French fries that day, his stomach felt bloated with nerves.

As he'd spoken to Alayna about the meteorite, he'd realized that he needed to alert the nearest, larger city of Helen for assistance. Without much scientific knowledge, and with an overactive imagination, he reasoned that meteorites might allow for contamination or lend themselves to viruses or microorganisms, and ultimately impact the ecosystem of the surrounding lands. In reality, he was just a small-town constable, with small-town habits and small-town opinions. He just needed a little, tiny bit of backup from the neighboring county.

The receptionist at the Helen police station picked up on the second ring. Her words were curt, stern, almost reminiscent of Lois, the Carterville mayor. "Hello, Helen police."

"Yes, hi," Clay began, lifting himself into a straight posture. His feet fell from the desk with a thunk. "My name is Clay Dobbs, and I'm sheriff over in Carterville. I was wondering if I might speak to your chief about a particular situation we have over here. We might need—"

"Please hold," the woman said, and silence fell on the other end of the line.

Clay waited in great anticipation, feeling unsure if calling out to another city was the right thing to do without first running it by Lois. In his years as sheriff of Carterville, he hadn't required much assistance. He'd prided himself on being the leader, on walking his people through every great tragedy, and on keeping the wretched kisses of one town floozy from passive or married men.

But meteorites? He Googled them quickly on his desktop, waiting as the other end buzzed with silence. Articles from NASA, *Time* magazine, and various science-based sites flooded his screen, asking terrible, wretched questions like, "Is Earth facing a threat of an asteroid collision?" and "Giant asteroid headed our way, but NASA says no worries." No worries? Beyond that he read that, as life possibly existed outside of Earth, meteorites could contain viruses and bacteria from other planets—ones that the people of Earth weren't accustomed to. Ones that could destroy them all.

Finally, after what seemed like an eternity, the woman on the other line called out his name. "Sheriff Clay? Clay Dobbs?" she said curtly.

"Yes. I'm still here," Clay said. He hoped his voice didn't shake through the receiver.

"I've spoken with the chief. He says that help has already been dispatched to your area."

Clay shifted his weight, his eyes still upon the screen before him. "I'm sorry. Help has already been dispatched? Just since I made this phone call? And he doesn't want to speak with me?" He felt the tension in his voice.

"No, sir. In fact, help was dispatched about an hour ago. They should arrive with you shortly. Unfortunately, the chief's in a meeting right now, but I can have him call you when he's available."

Clay's mind buzzed. Something was incredibly off. How could Helen have known about the meteorite? And if they didn't know about it, what were they sending help for? Besides the fire, nothing else had occurred to justify such a quick, if not premature, response. Nothing that he recalled, anyway. And Clay's mind was generally sharp. He swept his fingers over the wrinkles in his forehead, finally answering the woman on the other line. "Sure. Have him call back when he can. Tell him thank you, I guess."

Clay hung up the phone and stretched his arms over his head before striding toward the window. His eyes danced over the horizon. The sky was far too calm, almost irritatingly so. Helen was on their way.

After a thought struck him, he ran to Alayna's office, and was breathless when he reached her. She was hovered over her paperwork, a pen in her hand. She smiled as he burst in.

"Thought you'd catch me in the middle of slacking off, didn't you?" she teased.

But Clay's face didn't break into its familiar grin. He raked his fingers through his hair, shaking his head. "You didn't call Helen about the meteorite, did you?" he asked her. "Or anything else?"

Alayna frowned, shaking her head. "No. Of course not," she said. "That's up to you. I wouldn't overstep." She paused, thinking. "Why. What's up?"

"They've already sent help," Clay said. His voice was soft, almost a whisper. "Like they already know we're in trouble."

Alayna dropped her pen. The pair stared at each other, faced with this terrible truth. Who had called Helen? Had it been someone in the town who didn't trust Sheriff Clay's actions or abilities? Had it been Lois herself? He quickly dismissed this thought after recalling their conversation that morning about discretion. Perhaps Darcy's father, certain that something was afoot?

"Damn it all to hell," Clay burst, which was quite out of character for him. His normally even-keeled temper suddenly took a left turn. "Lois is going to have a conniption when she hears that word has leaked out somehow." Clay sighed heavily, trying to level his mood out. "I think I'm going to order something real to eat. Maybe I just can't think straight. You know?"

"Order me a sub sandwich," Alayna affirmed. "Otherwise, I might collapse in this office. And I know you need me. You're getting up there in age, after all." She winked at him, trying to spring their playfulness back to life.

But Clay gave her just a brief nod before returning to his office, feeling like the world had tilted just a little bit off. And he was left to figure out what was going to happen next.

9.

Cliff Henderson stared at his hands helplessly as he sat on the jail cell's only bench. Feeling his stomach quake within, he shuddered uncontrollably. It was nearly three in the afternoon, and he still hadn't used his allotted phone call out of fear that nobody would answer. He didn't want to acknowledge the fact that after nearly nine months in Carterville, he was alone. It was as if he was a foreigner in a far-off land. He was only half correct.

He'd gotten drunk and, in turn, too rowdy. And this time, he'd landed himself in an unfamiliar jail cell. Despite having a relative fondness for the drink, he had the unequivocal inability to embrace loneliness.

The previous evening's antics were blurry at best. He remembered feeling the tremors in his chest, and then the coughing fits as he wrapped up his shift. He'd stripped himself of his white coat and gloves and glared at his own reflection in the bathroom mirror, feeling the onset of flu alongside sheer, unadulterated solitude. The familiar creep had been present within him for nearly a decade, and he knew just the ticket for release.

Cliff had marched to the local bar at around nine in the evening, hearing the roar of the local football team's crowd down the street. He'd spit upon the ground, feeling a sudden rush of hatred for their kind. The men and women who always belonged—and always would—were the cheerleaders, the football players, the popular ones. It never changed. He'd always been a freak scientist. He wouldn't be anything else. Ever.

He'd eased into the local bar, collapsing upon the barstool and ordering a whisky. Or was it a double? He hadn't eaten since he lost his appetite, most certainly caused from the unexpected off-gassing that had overcome the lab. Of course, the rest of the town thought he worked at Moe's Candy. As if a town like this could support an abundance of truffles.

And so, because of his experimentation, he drank on an empty stomach, feeling his eyesight grow blurry as the night swept on.

Then, around midnight, Trudy had come in, all legs and thin arms and big breasts and fluttering eyelashes. He remembered flirting with her and tossing his arm around her, feeling like she was the only person he'd ever known his entire life. It was strangely pathetic.

He remembered feeling that violent anger toward her when she'd leaned toward the other woman at the bar and kissed her. Was Trudy a lesbian? He didn't care; he didn't mind lesbians. He just didn't want to bark up the wrong tree. The moment Trudy finished her face sucking, the woman she'd kissed called the police, irate, and he'd begun to scream at her. "I THOUGHT THIS WAS IT FOR US. I THOUGHT WE WERE GOING HOME TOGETHER."

As the memories of his own voice rang through his head, regret sputtered through him. And as he fell into it, he felt his stomach constrict. His eyes opened wide as he realized, all at once, that he was going to vomit.

"Shit," he said. He lunged for the toilet and wrapped his hands around the cold steel, feeling the vomit erupt from the depths of his body. Kyle, the officer who had picked both him and Trudy up the night before, shifted in his chair on the other side of the cell bars.

"You okay?" he called.

"Sure," Cliff spat. "Probably just the hangover."

"You were pretty messed up when I got to you," Kyle affirmed. He flipped a page in his newspaper.

Before Cliff could agree, before he could inquire when he could go home, the vomit was coursing through him once more. His eyes were wide, panicked. He felt as if his brain was burning. As he retched again, he noted that the toilet was filling with blood. He hadn't eaten in nearly a day. He had nothing left. Was this a side effect from his experiment? No. Surely he'd been careful enough. Surely he'd followed best lab practices.

But that wasn't always like him. Not at all—not in his past. In school he'd been written up many times for being lazy with his techniques, never washing his hands enough, always using dirty pipettes. It hadn't mattered then. He hadn't thought it really mattered now.

Shit.

Then, all at once, Cliff began to convulse, his limbs thrashing violently. He turned toward Kyle, who now stood erect, his paper in a heap at his feet. "Cliff?" he called. "Cliff, should I call the doctor?"

Cliff wasn't responding. Not anymore. Kyle tapped the buzzer, alerting someone, anyone else in the station that he needed assistance. Kyle's bright, youthful eyes hadn't seen anything so fierce before.

Cliff's actions bordered on the demonic, his body thrusting against the jail cell bars now. He was bludgeoning his cheeks. Blood spurted from his mouth, from gashes near his eyebrows and chin. He no longer looked human.

10.

Clay was hunched over his wastebasket. After inhaling his takeout lunch, his stomach had turned over, and he'd spent the better part of the previous thirty minutes retching. His stomach clenched violently. Then, suddenly, the station's intercom alert drowned out the sound of his guttural heaving. He wiped his lips, listening to the resounding alarm.

"If anyone's out there, I need help! Damn it, I need help right now!"

He ripped himself from his wastebasket the moment that he recognized Kyle's voice. What could he need? As far as Clay could remember, he was babysitting the lone person in the jail cell. That guy who manned the candy store. What could be so difficult with that?

But Clay was the epitome of diligence. He stood, swiped the last fleck of vomit from his lips, and marched toward lockup, his hand upon his gun. He couldn't allow the troops to know he was out of sorts. Not with everything going on.

When Clay reached the detention block, Kyle was poised before the bars, his hand upon his own gun. The candy man, Cliff, jerked forward in violent spasms. Bloody vomit spurt from his mouth. Clay yelled out to Kyle, feeling panicked. "What the hell's going on?"

Kyle was aghast. He took a step to the side, allowing Clay full view of the thrashing man. Cliff's head was lacerated at nearly every point on his forehead and near his ears, and a strange, purple substance oozed down his face. His eyes looked crazed, alien.

"CLIFF? CAN YOU HEAR ME?" Clay called to him, bending at the waist, unsure of the strength of his bowel control. He couldn't feel his spinning stomach any longer, but that didn't mean a thing. "CLIFF. GET AHOLD OF YOURSELF."

But Cliff continued to thrash frenetically. Clay reached toward the side desk, grabbing a Taser from the third drawer. He lifted it toward the crazed man and tried to spark him, tried to make him stop. But Cliff's spasms became more violent by the moment. A forceful head butt against the cell bar exploded the skin above his eyebrow, exposing bits of skeleton.

"STOP!" Clay cried out, still holding the Taser. He couldn't believe the man couldn't sense it. Perhaps he was having a seizure? It couldn't be an elaborate ruse at this point. It seemed medical. It seemed homicidal.

Moments later, with chunks of bone and blood dripping down the jail cell bars, Cliff fell to the ground. He was unconscious. He lay in a heap, his left arm abnormally reaching toward the far wall. He looked dead.

"Oh my god. Hand me the keys," Clay called, grabbing them from Kyle. He slotted the key into the jail cell hurriedly, adding, "And call the ambulance!"

The cell door opened slowly, with an ominous creak. And the moment it was wide enough to allow

Clay's entrance, everything seemed to explode. The man splayed before him sprung up, crazed, almost flying. His mouth opened, revealing sharp, bloodied teeth. He flailed his arms toward Clay with the intent to destroy—with inhuman tendencies—Clay was sure of it.

Instinctively, Clay reached for his gun. He pulled it up, shooting Cliff once in the chest. Clay blinked rapidly, watching as the beast recoiled backward from the force of the impact. Cliff lifted his bloodied hands toward his chest, his raving eyes still upon Clay. He heaved. And then, like a monster in a film, he lurched forward. The impact of the bullet hadn't destroyed him. Not for good.

Clay took a defensive stance, and in the final moment, he lifted his gun to the candy man's head and shot a bullet between his eyes, blasting his brains across the bricks of the jail cell wall. Cliff Henderson flung back and became a collection of bones and limbs and fat. He was a mound. He was nothing.

11.

Clay breathed heavily, questioning what he saw before him. His sight was momentarily obscured by Cliff's spattered blood, but a quick wipe with his free hand and his vision cleared. His eyes turned from the gun to the dead man and then toward Kyle. Kyle still held the phone in his hand. He was visibly shaking.

"Sheriff—" Kyle began, shaking his head. "What the fuck was—"

"I don't know, Kyle," Clay whispered. He felt the adrenaline drain from his muscles and brain. He was strangely empty, almost without awareness. "He hadn't been acting like this all day?"

Kyle shook his head. "I—I picked him up with Trudy last night," he said. He moved forward, looking at the man with morbid curiosity. "He was just drunk, Clay. He wasn't anything special. He wasn't sick, not that I could tell."

Alayna burst into the detention block, her gun drawn and ready for action. She quickly scanned the room, her eyes resting on Clay's pale form standing over a dead body.

"What happened?" she gasped as she moved into the crowded cell. The moment she saw Cliff's ravaged face, she took a quick step back and averted her eyes.

"I—I'm not sure. Kyle says he was fine just

before, but then he went crazy," Clay began.

"It's like a switch went off inside him. One moment we were talking, and then the next, he turned into this . . . zombie-like monster," Kyle added.

An eerie silence settled in the block, and seconds later, Alayna's complexion turned green and she rushed from the cell, her hand covering her mouth.

Clay left the cell, feeling the weight of the death upon his shoulders. He exited the station, allowing the sun to fall upon his cheeks. Absentmindedly, he reholstered his gun. He'd never killed anyone before. He'd always wondered about it, what it would mean to erase someone's name from existence. But he hadn't craved it. He was in the business of saving people, not destroying them.

Moments later Kyle appeared beside him. He peered at him like a son looked upon his commanding father. He was similar to Maia, only a few years older. A few years wiser.

"You did the right thing," Kyle said, sniffing. "Seriously. He was out to kill you."

"Let's just get the coroner out here," Clay said. He appreciated Kyle's words, but he didn't want to acknowledge them. He wanted to move toward understanding. He didn't want to dwell on this new, confusing, terrible feeling. He wanted answers.

"Why don't you go home and get cleaned up, then," Kyle said. "We can handle things for a bit."

But Clay shook his head, recognizing that in his normally peaceful town, two people had now died in less than twenty-four hours. "I have to stay," he said. "I have a change of clothes. I always do."

12.

Later, Clay and Alayna sat in his office. Silence seemed impenetrable as their thoughts turned wild within them.

"Are you feeling any better?" Clay asked, tapping his fingers absentmindedly. "Your stomach, I mean."

"Ah, my lunch in reverse," Alayna exhaled sharply. "I forgot about it, really. Everything feels . . . wrong. Doesn't it to you?"

Clay swiped his fingers through his hair, remembering the frenzy of Cliff's limbs. "Damn it, Alayna. He didn't even register that I was tasing him. It seemed like he was so far away. And then, when he came at me—" He shook his head, furrowing his brow. "I'd only met him once or twice. I took Maia in to buy some chocolate maybe two months ago. He seemed like a regular guy, if a bit withdrawn and disorganized. And then, he's picked up for being disorderly last night. Do you think he was on drugs?" His words came fast.

"I've never seen a drug impact somebody like that," Alayna whispered. "Never in all my years."

"Granted, maybe the people in Helen have," Clay offered. "We're just a small town here. I've spent no more than three or four days at a time in any other city. It's all just too much for me." He shuddered, remembering marching through the New York streets on a vacation with Valerie nearly five years before. He'd only felt solid, safe when they'd returned back to their Carterville home. He'd wrapped himself tightly in his private little hamlet, facing the truth: he wasn't cut out for any other kind of life.

"It has to be a coincidence, right?" Alayna said then. "With this meteorite crashing down. And now, with Cliff acting like a maniac—"

"I'm sure they're not related," Clay stammered. "The science isn't there. Plus, Cliff was miles away from the meteorite, locked in the jail cell. If he was affected by it, then everyone around us should be too."

"Right," Alayna said. Her voice sounded small, far away.

As they sat in the silence, they both sensed a sudden trembling beneath their feet. Clay lifted his hands to the desk, noting that the wood itself was vibrating. He eyed Alayna, unsure if he was truly going crazy this time.

"Do you feel that?"

"I do," Alayna said.

They rose from their seats and made their way toward the front office of the station, noting that more of the staff had also deserted their positions. They formed a line outside the station, their arms crossed, gazing out at the horizon. Clay stood, his boots shoulder width apart, glaring into the sunlight. Far down Highway 77, which became Main Street as it went through town, he saw the haze of several large, menacing vehicles. He tapped his hand against his revolver, noting it was still flecked with Cliff's blood. He shivered.

Alayna whispered toward him, anxious for no one else to hear. "What the hell is that?"

13.

As the caravan of vehicles grew closer, more townspeople appeared from their homes and shops, glaring out into the distance. Several gasped, but most looked firm, stoic, with the "come what may" mentality of good provincial people.

Finally, when the convoy was closer, rolling down the dry and dusty pavement, Clay caught the military insignia on several of the vehicles. A large tank trailed them, pointing a massive gun toward the center of the town square. Clay pushed through the crowd on Main Street, standing in the center of the road, his chin high. He sensed that this was the "backup" from Helen. But why on earth had they sent the military, rather than a few cop cars and perhaps some scientists who would investigate the meteorite? None of it made sense.

Alayna hurried to his side and stood with him, her fingers tapping lightly on her own gun. As the military slowed to a crawl, Clay's mind flashed to images of his daughter and wife.

The procession formed a sturdy line between the early twentieth-century buildings and shops. Clay could see slight movement in the driver's seats of the vehicles but still clung to his gun, realizing all of the townspeople had their eyes upon him.

In that moment, one of the transport's doors

burst open, revealing a large combat boot, followed by a sturdy, long leg. A military man emerged: all seven feet tall of him, his hair short and cropped, almost Nazi-like, and his blue eyes flashing. He marched toward Clay, lifting his hand to his brow and saluting him. He then turned toward the expectant station's staff. They peered at him like bunny rabbits about to be slaughtered.

"Staff of Carterville Sheriff's Department, thank you for welcoming me," he barked, his voice harsh. "My name is Colonel Scott Wallace. I like to keep a tight ship around here, and if you follow my orders to a *T*, we won't have a moment's problem. Is that clear?"

Clay felt mass confusion deep within, laced with fits of anger. The man towered over him, and yet he felt a longing to reach up and punch him across the face, then ask him who the hell he thought he was. What made him think he could come toward his people, his staff, and begin bossing them around?

Clay strode forward, clearing his throat. He felt like a child, exerting his force on the playground. "Excuse me," he said. "I'm Sheriff Clay Dobbs. What's going on here?"

Wallace's yellow eyebrows shot upward. He smirked, assessing Clay. But Clay held his ground, bursting with resentment. He didn't take orders from anyone but Lois, the mayor. And even then, he wasn't too happy about it when it happened. He needed time to form a strategy. Or at the very least, he wanted to be treated with respect as he worked alongside this out-of-towner.

"I see," Wallace said. "You're the sheriff around here. I understand that you made a call to the city of Helen, describing a need for some backup. Is that correct?"

The curious staff turned their gaze toward Clay. Clay felt small. But he raised his chin still higher, glaring this man in the eye. "That's correct. Backup. Which, I believe, has quite a different definition than you think it does."

Wallace scoffed. "I see. So you think you and your ragtag crew can really monitor this town after what's happened?" he said.

"What exactly do you know?" Clay asked. "When I called Helen to explain, they didn't even take my call. They just said help was on its way. Why send what looks like an entire military detachment for a simple meteor impact?"

The colonel cleared his throat and raised his head even higher, averting his gaze to the surrounding townspeople. "Because you never can be too careful. Besides, do you think you can keep your little town safe from all that's out there waiting for you?" He gave a knowing grin. "Because I think there's a lot you don't know, Sheriff."

Clay gripped his hands together so tightly that his nails nearly drew blood. "I'm sorry to tell you, sir, that you're out of your turf and out of line."

Wallace raised his massive hands. "I see," he said gruffly. "I do. And, I suppose, for the time being, you can keep your little church-town." He gestured toward the post office, the bank, making a mockery of it. "But in the meantime, I think we have to make a compromise. For the safety of your people."

Clay tilted his head. He felt a compromise wouldn't rectify his problem. He wanted to take this man inside, to demand answers. But in this public setting, with Alayna and Jean and the bank staff and several girls from the local school all switching their eyes from him to the colonel and back to him, he couldn't back down.

"Depends on the compromise," Clay said.

"I suppose it's more of an order, then," Wallace corrected. "We're going to hold a perimeter around Carterville. We're aware of the incident at the farmhouse and require a brief quarantine, until the issue at hand has been completely investigated. Do you understand?"

Clay remembered the heat of that meteorite upon his cheeks. He felt his stomach lurch within him. He'd vomited both his lunch and those drive-thru French fries, and still something within him yearned to escape.

"That's fine," Alayna said then, interrupting the conversation. "Please. Make your perimeter. I'm sure it can't hurt. And we'll be happy to help in any way we can."

Wallace turned his eyes toward the deputy. "Seems your little woman here has a bit more sense than you do, Sheriff," he said. He clapped his hands together, the sound echoing against the brick side of the station and then from the bank to the school to the city apartment block. "Move out, team," he said.

The military procession turned from the city center and spread out to all corners of Carterville to form a perimeter. Clay watched them go, his heart aching. Alayna's fingers gripped his elbow, assuring him that this would be over soon. They watched Colonel Wallace withdraw back to his own vehicle, salute, and promise, "I'll be back here soon to talk shop with you, Clay." He tapped his nose. "Just you wait. We'll be fast friends. I promise."

Clay didn't wait for the convoy to clear completely from Main Street. He stomped into the station, noting the smell that weaved through the air in the hours after Cliff's death. He collapsed into his office chair, gripping the telephone receiver. He had to call Lois, but he dreaded yet another confrontation. He sat in the shadows, understanding that, at least for a little while, his world wouldn't look precisely right. They meteorite had come for them all. It had chosen them, like fate. And now, he had to act with his townspeople's best interests in mind. Which meant, he supposed, he'd have to bend his confidence. He'd have to cower at the feet of this wretched man. He'd have to find a purpose in that, if only to protect the livelihood of the people he loved the most.

Clay reached out and dialed Lois's private number.

14.

Mayor Lois Washington returned Clay's call less than an hour after Colonel Wallace had swept through the town. Clay felt the dread in his voice as he answered. "Sheriff Dobbs."

"I hear you've met our savior, Lord Wallace," Lois said, her voice slicing through the air. This was no longer the woman who judged the baby animal contest in the summertime or cut the ribbon on his daughter's apple cider sale in autumn, ten years before. This was a woman of purpose. This was the woman he'd met earlier that morning. The woman who had asked him to keep the investigation quiet.

"They really made an entrance," Clay offered, leaning back heavily upon the headrest. "Mind telling me what this is all about?"

"I don't know much," Lois said nervously, "but what I do know is, something's happening in this town. And they know the precise mechanism to keep us safe. So why not let them?"

Clay bit his tongue.

"Oh, I know. I know. You just hate taking orders. But hear this order from me," Lois said. "There is so much more that will become clear in time, and as soon as I can say, you'll be the first to know. But until then, know that this will blow over soon. Just stay strong. Won't you?"

The old woman sounded so much like his mother before her death: confident, optimistic, bright. He stuttered a brief agreement before hearing the final order.

"I think you should go visit Darcy Crawford," Lois said then. "I really think she deserves your support."

"Alayna went out this morning, when I met you at the diner," Clay explained. He stared at the dirt on his boots, remembering the early morning's inspection of the farmhouse and barn.

"I know that," Lois said, irritated. "But she and her father are important to this town. And I know, more than anyone, how much this town means to you. It's been your life for far too long to sit around and mope."

"You're getting all sentimental on me, Lois," Clay said, feeling blood pump in his veins once more. The old mayor was right. "I suppose I could head over there. I don't know what else I'll do here at the office, besides worry about what Colonel Wallace and his band of no-goods are doing at the perimeter."

"That's the spirit," Lois said. "Hey. I have to run to a meeting. But we'll speak soon."

A meeting on a Saturday? Clay wondered. "Yeah, sure."

"And Clay?" she offered, her voice hesitant.

"What is it, Lois?"

"Be careful."

15.

Clay gave a brief good-bye to Alayna before bounding away from the station, already feeling like the day wouldn't end. It was only five in the afternoon, and he didn't sense leaving his post anytime soon, or slipping out of his treacherous shoes. Jesus. He stretched his toes within the thick, unforgiving material. He ached.

He pulled into the lot at the hospital, parking close to the emergency room. As he walked, he sensed questioning eyes upon him. He bowed his head in greeting to several nurses who stood outside with cigarettes between their lips. They looked harried, their eyes bloodshot and red. "Afternoon, ladies," he said.

A nurse at the waiting station led him to Darcy's room. He felt outside of himself as his boots squeaked on the linoleum floor. As gurneys pushed past him, he realized he didn't fully recognize everyone who passed. These were the people he was meant to care for. These were the people he planned to protect. And yet they were invisible, anonymous.

The moment Clay saw Darcy in the hospital bed, his breath caught sharp in his throat. Her hair wove around her face, creating a kind of dark cloud. And her eyelashes fluttered at her red-tinged cheeks, giving her an angelic appearance. Her thin wrists looked unsuited to do any labor: like tiny, mouse wrists, broken with an ounce of weight. He couldn't imagine how this girl could endure a brief windstorm, let alone survive the meteorite.

Beside the bed sat Mack Crawford, her father—a man Clay had been rather friendly with over the years. Mack's back was curved, his elbows upon his knees. He looked like he was weeping, shuddering with tears.

Clay reached toward him, nearly ready to touch his shoulder, to offer support. But immediately the man lurched back with a violent motion. His eyes were red, his skin splotchy. He popped his lips in a moment of recognition.

"Sheriff," he said gruffly.

"Mack. Are you doing all right?" Clay asked, his voice tentative. He instantly noticed how profusely Mack was perspiring. "You don't look too well. Do you have the flu or—"

Mack stood up and began pacing, interrupting Clay. His boots rattled across the floor and his words came spastically. "Jesus, Clay. I wish everyone would stop getting on my case about this. I'm fucking fine," Mack said. He slapped an open palm on an adjacent wall. The sound echoed throughout the room and rang through Clay's ears. He eased back, standing in the doorway.

Mack continued. "All this. Darcy being in the hospital. I lost the entire farm. Do you know how hard I've worked for that farm? The barn and the house? It's all I have!"

"The fields are mostly fine," Clay offered. "I stopped there this morning. It was bad luck, for sure, but you haven't lost your daughter. That's what's most important, isn't it?"

Mack continued to pace, wringing his hands. Sweat continued to pour, staining his shirt in splotches beneath his armpits. "If I could only get some space," he sputtered. "I just wish everyone would leave me alone."

Clay rested his hands on his hips, mentally stepping away from the grieving man and his unconscious daughter. He remembered the panic in Cliff's eyes back at the jail cell and drew a direct comparison to Mack, who was all but thrashing between him and the hospital bed. He imagined the possibility of Mack's violent thrusts coming down upon Darcy, his own daughter.

He spoke tentatively. "Listen. I know you aren't feeling well, Mack. Just admit it to yourself and head to a hotel. Get some sleep. We all know you need it. And the nurses will call you the minute your daughter wakes up."

Mack burst forward, then, sending his fist to the base of Clay's chin. He growled slightly, the whites of his eyes showing jaundice yellow. "Don't you fucking tell me what to do," he spat. "You get out of here."

The sheriff's instinct took over once more, forcing him to wrap his arms around this manic man who was on the edge. He pushed Mack to the ground, beside his sleeping daughter's form, and held him between his calves before reaching back and tugging his cuffs from his pocket. He cuffed him, surprised at the strength in the forty-something man, nearly causing him to topple toward the ground.

"Easy, there," Clay said, scarcely believing what he was doing. Mack wasn't fully berserk, not like Cliff had been. But as Clay began to help the man to his feet, Mack heaved back and vomited all over the linoleum. The smell was wretched, curdling in Clay's nose. But still, he held fast to Mack's upper bicep, feeling his straining strength.

"You feel better?" he asked.

Mack heaved several breaths, clearly unable to answer. He shot himself back to his feet, sputtering with anger. He gave a final look to his daughter before asking, "So. Where the fuck you gonna take me now, Mr. Sheriff?" His eyes were dark over the yellow background. And his skin seemed off, like the inside of a sour grape.

"We'll head back to the station for now," Clay said, trying to sound sure of himself. But in reality, the strangeness of the day made his every movement seem fictional. He ached for his bed.

Clay gave a final glance to Darcy, then led her father from the room.

16.

Mack thrashed several times as they marched through the hallway before finally giving up and walking slowly, dispassionately, his arms hanging behind his back in their cuffs.

Clay had half a mind to let him free in that moment. Perhaps he was truly just upset about his daughter. Perhaps he was truly a grieving father, yearning to be left alone.

But the moment Mack's skin felt the assault of sunlight outside the hospital, he began to toss himself violently once more. He screamed wretchedly, highlighting the wrinkles on his forehead, his cheeks, around his eyes. Clay waffled around him, catching him at his shoulders, trying to calm him.

"Mack! Hey! It's all right, buddy!" But his words sounded weak and tired in the face of such anger. Clay felt himself staggering left, then right as he clung to him, moving with each of Mack's insane thrusts. He was nearly pummeled to the ground but soon righted himself, finding the strength to stand firm in his boots.

Just as Clay assumed Mack would never halt this violence, that he would have to carry him the rest of the way to his sheriff's car, he heard a loud engine revving behind him. His heart sank with intense fear. His fingertips dipped deeper into Mack's biceps, hoping he was wrong. That the sound was nothing. Just another farmer in a loud truck.

But the footfalls behind him told him a different story. The angry, obnoxious voice coiled within his ears, chilling Clay to the bone.

"Well, well. Sheriff Dobbs. What in the world do we have here?" Colonel Wallace drawled, assessing Mack's ominous behavior. "Seems rather peculiar to me. Not just like a man who almost lost his daughter today. But more like a man on the brink of insanity. Wouldn't you agree?"

Clay maintained his steady posture, turning his head so that only his stark profile showed to Wallace, hoping to retain control. "He's just upset," he affirmed. "He's had a hard day."

As if on cue, Mack squealed wildly, like a pig. He thrust himself so violently in Clay's arms that Clay lost his hold. Mack stumbled backward, nearly tossing himself in front of an ambulance, hightailing it through the crunching pavement. From this distance, Clay sensed the danger in this man. He sensed that he'd crossed over the line, much closer to the behavior exhibited by Cliff earlier that afternoon.

Wallace smacked his hands together, throwing an echo across the hospital's brick wall. On this cue, three of his men marched forward and grasped Mack Crawford by the arm, the leg, the torso, and then flung him in the back of one of their transports, still handcuffed. He screamed like a caged animal.

"What do you expect you can do with him that I wasn't already going to?" Clay demanded, leaning toward the colonel.

"He'll be quarantined for evaluation," Wallace said, sniffing. "It's a technique we often use in these situations."

"You do realize that it's probably just the flu," Clay said hopefully. "Faced with the condition of his daughter and the loss of his farm, he's just a little manic."

"Leave your diagnosis attempts to the professionals. And please, Sheriff, if you see anyone else exhibiting these symptoms, send them our way. We have our quarantine facility set up just outside of town, and we have the tools and the know-how to deal with this."

"Is that an order?" Clay challenged, still hearing Mack fighting himself in the back of the transport. Clay swallowed, almost thankful not to have Mack's fate on his hands. Not like Cliff. He couldn't handle that twice in one day.

"Sure is," Wallace said, stretching a smile across his face. "You don't want to destroy one of your fellow men in the process, now, do you?" He turned his eyes back to his soldiers, who stood in a straight line, their eyes toward him. "Let's move out, boys. Lucky we were in the neighborhood, eh?"

They stomped back to their vehicles and sped from the parking lot, leaving Clay alone, staring into the ether. He sensed that the life he'd woken up to, with his wife and daughter in his quaint, country home, might very well be a figment from his past. But he couldn't think about that now. He had to move beyond this helpless feeling and get to the bottom of this wretched day. What the fuck was going on?

And for all their pomp, he wasn't entirely sure that Colonel Wallace and his troops had all the answers.

17.

Clay paced his office hours later, his hands clasped behind his back. Alayna sat with her feet upon his desk, her fingers jittering as she thought aloud.

"When I saw Mack at the hospital, he was exhibiting these same symptoms," she said again. "And it seems that Darcy had similar signs. But she wasn't ranting and raving like you say Mack was." She paused, gazing out the window. "Where do you think they took him?"

"Colonel Wallace said the facility was set up just outside of town. Probably just over the county line and out of our reach." Clay threw up a bewildered shrug. He felt his stomach lurch within him once more and nearly hacked into the trash can. He couldn't decide if he actually felt ill or if the stress of the day had its hands around his neck. He absentmindedly scratched at some scaly skin on his forehead. His hand returned to his side trailing several strands of his salt-and-pepper hair. He searched his fingers, aghast, and noted that on his forearm were the beginnings of some lesions, lying just beneath the surface of his skin. He dropped his arm back down, noting that Alayna had turned toward him.

"What was that?" she asked.

"Nothing. I hit my arm on a burner the other day," Clay lied. He felt a bead of sweat form at his temple.

Alayna bought it easily. She had no reason not to trust him. She cracked her knuckles and bound back into the discourse, leaving Clay with his roving thoughts.

"Anyway. With the military presence, the mood in this town has really taken a nose dive. Don't you think all the activity is overkill? It's making the natives uneasy. We had almost ten people in the station when you were gone, demanding answers about all the transports and the tank. We're a small town, here, you know? I just don't think we need all this."

Clay nodded, gliding a hand over his forearm, sensing that the lesion was somehow related. He was frightened, but he couldn't show it. "We'll take steps to get them out of town and get Mack some actual medical attention. Imagine. I'm sure they've just thrown him in some kind of cage until he stops showing symptoms. That could kill a guy."

In that moment, the door swung open, revealing the tiny, angular face of Mayor Washington. She breathed quickly, like a tiny bird. She lifted a paper into the air and flung it across Clay's desk, pointing at the headline spread across the page.

"Meteorites and Militia: The Day Carterville Went Crazy." Beside the headline was a photo of Colonel Wallace, his face intense and demanding, and Clay. His own presence in the photo seemed trivial in comparison—not a person you'd allow to watch over your town, let alone your dog for the weekend. Not one of Clay's best photogenic moments.

He hadn't expected this. "They printed a special

edition in the middle of a Saturday?" he said, remembering the faces at the Carterville Gazette. They'd turned on him.

"It doesn't matter," Lois said, her head rigid. "What matters is, we need to do something about the rumors floating around this town. People have watched too many sci-fi movies, and now they're running rampant with all these postapocalyptic thoughts. On my walk here, I saw two mothers weeping over their strollers, like it was the end of the world. Clay, we have to do something. We can't have the entire town go mad as we sit idle."

Clay's mind raced. Alayna began to stutter an answer, but he held up his hand, halting her. "Listen, Lois, I can't control what people think. Sure, I get why they're scared. Heck, I didn't know how much 'assistance' Helen was going to send over when I requested it. They dispatched an entire military outfit."

Lois dropped her eyes and stared at the newspaper, visibly shaking.

"But we'll get things under control," Clay continued. "Sure, we've lost a few good people today. But give my team some time to figure things out, and if we're lucky, we won't lose any more." Clay wasn't entirely sure how they'd follow through on his words, but he had confidence in each and every deputy in his department. A slight grin stretched across his face.

Lois answered immediately. "I suppose you haven't heard about the new cases, then?"

Clay's jaw dropped. "I'm—I'm sorry?"

"The military has quarantined five more people, all exhibiting similar symptoms. First, it's the sweats," Lois said, "followed closely by uncontrolled vomiting before it devolves into a kind of animalistic, crazed behavior during which they forget who they are and where they came from."

Clay nodded, remembering the eyes of both Cliff and Mack. "So the military believes it's all related to the meteorite?" he asked, feeling small beads of sweat form once more at his hairline. He flicked them away, hoping Lois didn't notice.

"Sure, maybe. They don't know its precise relation, but that whatever this 'virus' is, it's contagious."

"Isn't this all a little premature?" Clay asked. "I know there are several cases of the flu running around town. Hell, Maia is fighting it off as we speak."

"Right now, no one is sure." Lois sniffed. "We have the makings of an epidemic on our hands. And if we're not careful, it'll overtake us all."

Alayna gasped and tilted her head back, clearly falling into the initial levels of grief. Clay could empathize. Carterville was his town. And he felt he was watching it sink into the sea.

"That leads me to my next question," Lois said. "Have either of you begun experiencing symptoms? I know that both of you have been around the Crawfords. Clay, you even saw the meteorite with your own damn eyes."

Clay shook his head almost imperceptibly. He could practically feel the hair leaping from his scalp. But he took an offensive path, his voice coming out almost in a growl. "Lois, you know we wouldn't endanger the people of this town. The moment we experience symptoms, we'll let you know. All right?"

Lois turned toward Alayna, who shook her head as well. No symptoms.

"Well, good," Lois said, pressing her hands

together as if to break out in a prayer. "Then I suppose we all have a job to do. Keep the peace as much as possible—"

"And what about the military? Allow them to keep up this horrid 'gathering up' of sick people?" Clay demanded. "We need to keep our town, Lois. We can't afford to give it up. The hospital can certainly handle whatever this it, wouldn't you agree?"

As he spoke, the door burst open once more, revealing the man of the hour: Colonel Wallace. He lifted his hand into the air and began to bark his words in such a deep, terrible pitch, it took a moment for Clay to wrap his mind around his meaning.

18.

"This town is falling into chaos," Wallace began. "We've picked up more locals exhibiting symptoms, fifteen in total at this point, and know that several more will fall to this illness."

"Colonel, aren't you exaggerating the situation just a bit?" Lois asked, straightening her posture and shifting her gaze upon the commander. "The sheriff has just informed me that there's widespread instances of influenza running amok. How can you be certain that everyone you've picked up isn't just suffering the common flu?"

Colonel Wallace blinked slowly, dramatically, showing his equivalent of rolling his eyes. "Mayor. Sheriff. My military has a plan, and this sheriff's office is frankly unqualified. I said I would allow you to retain leadership of this town, but now, I am rescinding that offer. This is far too dangerous. We need to quarantine everyone that is showing signs of contamination. A forced evacuation is imperative, as we need to release a chemical propellant to kill this thing. We're taking the town from you. It's ours now," his voice boomed.

In the brief moment of silence after Wallace's speech, Lois stepped forward, glaring at him. In his feverish mind, Clay expected Lois to agree with the colonel. Morale was at an all-time low, and Colonel

Wallace was offering ready answers.

But Lois surprised him. "You'll take this town away from the sheriff's office over my dead body," she spat, stabbing her finger toward his colossal frame. "Fifteen flu-like cases is hardly an epidemic," she said, contradicting her own words from just minutes earlier. "My medical staff and law enforcement are perfectly capable of doing their job, and I wouldn't have it any other way."

Her voice hung in the air. The tension in the room was high. Clay felt an abrupt cough churning through his lungs, but he held it in, taking deep, controlled breaths. Now wasn't the time to reveal his illness.

"Don't get me wrong," Lois continued. "I agree, for safety reasons, that an evacuation is necessary. But I'm not about to let you round up my residents like a pack of rabid dogs."

"The longer you wait, the more chance this thing can spiral out of control."

Lois lifted her chin as if in deep contemplation. "All right. How about we make this evacuation happen over the next twenty-four hours? Is that fast enough for you?"

"It's a start. At least let us quarantine anyone showing infection. If we can curtail the spread now, the better off everyone will be."

She turned suddenly toward Clay, her face stern, pointed. "Sheriff Dobbs, do you have any problem with that?"

Clay shook his head. He was speechless, his tongue lost somewhere in his mouth. He hoped that Maia didn't have the full-blown flu yet, otherwise she'd be rounded up in the wrong group.

Wallace took a step back, giving the room a bit

more air. "Regardless, I think you're making a big mistake not letting my outfit take over," he said, his voice gruff.

"I'm not," Lois insisted. "I've seen my people handle some of the most dastardly situations. We've got this one. Now. Get back to whatever hole you crawled out of."

"You have to let the people know what's going on," Wallace continued, barreling over her words. "You can't leave them in the dark like this. People are sick." His eyes roved toward Clay, assessing his complexion. "It isn't fair. It isn't politically sound. You, as mayor, should know that. You should let them know their options. You should let them know we can defeat this."

Lois tilted her head, digesting each of his words. "All right," she said. "We'll have a town hall meeting this evening. We can address the current issues then. Explain the reality of the meteorite, and then calm everyone down. The last thing we need on our hands are several thousand people panicked and running through the streets. Don't you agree, Colonel?"

Wallace bowed his head, tapping his boot upon the wooden floor. He seemed childlike, earnest, in that moment. "Sure, Mayor. I suppose I won't overstep quite yet. But the moment this turns into a complete and utter—"

Lois halted him. "We've got this. Like I said. We'll formulate a plan and announce it tonight." Her voice dominated over him, causing Wallace to turn back toward the station entrance and retreat to his corps. He left Alayna, Lois, and Clay alone in the shadowed office, each spinning in a separate world of fears and anxieties.

Had they made the right decision, taking this

into their own hands?

19.

At eight-thirty that evening, Clay found himself standing at the entrance of the massive Protestant church on the square, where they held the occasional town meeting. He held his hands upon his waist, feeling himself waver slightly from fatigue. He'd covered his lesions with long sleeves to avoid any potential questioning. Jesus. What was he going to do?

Alayna appeared before him then. She gave him a slight smile, gesturing toward the first of many cars that meandered down Main Street. "I guess this is it, huh?" she said, her voice light. "At least I finally made it to deputy status. Although, I think I could have made a really great sheriff." She winked.

"The beginning of an unexpected interruption? Yes. Is this the end? I don't think so. Lois assures me that everything will be all right," Clay said. "Besides, I think you're just trying to angle for my job again."

Alayna smiled before shoving her elbow into Clay's side playfully.

They'd sent out messengers to all areas of town, along with phone alerts, ensuring that everyone knew about the town meeting. He'd called Valerie after Wallace had left his office, alerting her about it and the meteorite. Her voice had sounded so smooth, so easy in his ears.

That is, until he'd told her about the happenings from throughout the day.

"What do you mean, an epidemic?" she'd spurt into the phone.

"We've got it under control, honey," Clay had sighed. "I'll explain more at the meeting. Will you bring Maia? I want to make sure you're both close."

"Jesus. This is serious, isn't it, Clay?" Valerie had whispered. "Should I pack?"

"Maybe," Clay offered. "But don't panic yet. We're in the beginning stages of some very routine actions. Trust me. Just because this hasn't happened to us before doesn't mean it hasn't happened to other people. Accidents and terrible events happen all the time. And people survive. They persevere."

But Clay noted that Valerie and Maia were two of the last to arrive at the town hall meeting, causing him to miss greeting them. He gave them a slight wave as they entered the back, behind several hundred townsfolk, and crunched into small holes in the final pew. Valerie made brief eye contact with him. He could tell she'd been crying.

Mayor Washington stood at the pulpit at the front of the room and lifted her hands, almost as if she were about to direct an orchestra. The mighty chorus of townspeople died down, allowing her to speak.

"People of Carterville," she began in her practiced, political voice—the one that had gotten her elected countless times. "It is with great sadness that I bring you together tonight. But it is with immense happiness that I can present a solution to all the terrible fears."

"FINALLY!" someone cried out from the back, his voice guttural and strange.

"That's right," Lois smiled. "As many of you probably know by now, a meteorite crashed into the Crawford barn last night, killing one of our youngest and brightest. Caleb. To his mother and father, Tasha and Jim, I give you my utmost love and empathy. Caleb will be missed."

In the front row, off to the right, a woman turned her face toward her husband's shoulder and shook violently with tears.

But Lois continued. "As a result of this meteorite, a strange illness has begun to sweep through the town. The illness is characterized by flu-like symptoms and hot flashes, and then, ultimately, violence to both one's self and others. Due to this illness, the military has resolved to quarantine many of the Carterville population, keeping them away from the rest of us. But ultimately, we are not safe here.

"The military, led by this man to my right, Colonel Scott Wallace, wants to do a forced evacuation and then release a chemical propellant with the intent to kill off the virus. If, of course, a virus is what this thing really is."

Across the crowd, faces broke into panicked expressions and eyes filled with tears. Someone had brought their dog, near the back, and the hound began to howl, exhibiting the very note of despair the entire town held.

"But, of course, this 'forced' evacuation is incredibly outside of your rights, as people of Carterville," Lois continued. "Any kind of force would ultimately result in violence. And for this reason, I urge for a voluntary evacuation. This is more appropriate for our small-town lifestyle. We do not force. We ask. We help. We join together."

In this pause, she gave a bright smile to the crowd. Clay noted that she was probably honing her next campaign, ensuring that she was the one who stepped up to the plate. The people of Carterville could trust her above everything. That she would use an opportunity like this for personal gain turned Clay's stomach over.

"I'd like to interrupt you," Colonel Wallace boomed from the side of the room. He strode forward, demanding the eyes of everyone in the room. "You see, the small-town atmosphere here in Carterville is exactly the problem," he said. "Everyone knows everyone else. And the spread of this virus, therefore, can escalate much quicker."

The crowd gasped once more. Fear filled the air. Clay felt he could hardly breathe. He watched as his daughter, Maia, brought her hand up to cover her mouth, shivering with anticipation. Everything in her life had flipped upside down. What was it she'd been mad about that morning? A teenage problem, in a teenage life that had virtually no meaning anymore.

"This is a dangerous situation," Wallace continued. "And until we understand how to stop this meteorite's virus, my plan is far more appropriate."

"And what, exactly, does your 'forced evacuation' look like?" Lois spat into the microphone. "Does it mean you go door to door with a bus and force everyone out of their homes? Because I really don't see how that would work. Especially not here. We're too proud a people."

"Well, if that's what it comes down to, yes," Wallace answered. "We need to stop the infection in its tracks. And I'm willing to do anything and everything in my power to do that."

The crowd erupted. Friends, relatives, and

neighbors bowed their heads to each other and began saying panicked words, making terrible, earnest plans. “He’s not going to take me from my home!” several spewed. “How dare he come in here and say this to us? Doesn’t he know who we are?”

As the panic rose, Clay watched as Lois took several tentative steps back from the pulpit. Her hands shook. She’d lost her grip. She looked tiny, like a child too frightened to leap from the diving board. And Clay knew, in that moment, that he had to do something. He had to find a way to lead.

20.

He stepped toward the pulpit and tapped on the microphone, causing the sound to boom out over the heads of the Carterville townspeople. "Hello!" he cried, slicing into their harried conversations. "Hello. Please listen. I think I have a better plan." His eyes danced across the crowd. To his right, he heard Colonel Wallace snort.

"I think we can all agree that this is an unforeseen tragedy," Clay said, his voice taking on a commanding tone. "But I'd like to give us all twelve hours to get out of town. Pack our bags with all our favorite belongings, make sure we have places to be, and drive our own cars out of town."

Wallace scoffed. "You'll have too many stragglers," he said. "People who refuse to leave their homes. People who won't make plans. And they won't take to this chemical propellant well at all. You'll be responsible for countless deaths."

The words hung in the air for several moments. Clay pondered, unsure, until he made eye contact with Alayna. She brimmed with pride.

"My deputy, Alayna, and I will remain in town and round up the remaining stragglers until everyone—and I mean everyone—is out of danger. And then, we'll get out ourselves, and Colonel Wallace here can release his chemical 'bomb.' Or whatever it is."

"Will it destroy our town?" someone cried out from below. She bounced a baby upon her knee.

"That's a great question. Colonel Wallace, is the bomb destructive?" Clay asked.

Wallace nodded slightly. His eyes looked far away, reluctant. "Sure. This 'chemical bomb', as you have erroneously quoined it, is nondestructive," he said. "It's a chemical propellant, as I said. The fumigation process should neutralize the virus without physically damaging any of the town's structures. Human exposure will most certainly be fatal, however, hence the urgency of the evac. After one month's time, everyone will be allowed back in their homes. And the town of Carterville can continue its regular, boring schedule."

Clay swept his hands to the sky, enacting a similar pose to Lois—almost prayerful. "Now I know this is going to be difficult for us," he began, "but I need you all to understand. We must fight for our town. We must fight to stay alive. And today, this requires us to leave. I want you all to start your journey home. Pack your bags, anything you'll need for the next month, including any medication, and get out of here."

"One more thing," Colonel Wallace said, silencing the frantic murmurs from the crowd. "For the chemical propellant to reach its full effectiveness, my scientists have informed me that the local cell phone towers would have to be deactivated. Therefore, beginning at eight tomorrow morning, none of you will have cellular service until you are out of town."

Clay noticed Colonel Wallace smirk ever so slightly at his latest ploy to undermine the town. Why the hell would the cell towers interfere with the fumigation?

All at once, the crowd erupted from their pews. They elbowed and scrambled their way toward the exit, grabbing on to their children's hands. Clay felt mildly content: he still had power over his people despite everything. And as he turned, he received a tiny, firm grin from the mayor. She mouthed, "Good job, Sheriff."

21.

As the church cleared, leaving only Clay, Alayna, Lois, and Colonel Wallace, Clay reached for the colonel's hand and shook it firmly. He felt an engrained sense of responsibility for his people, alongside a fluttering of cockiness. He'd beaten Wallace at his military game. And everything was going to be all right. Hopefully.

"We'll see how this goes," Wallace said gruffly. He stomped from the church's side entrance and slipped a cigarette from his pocket, popping it between his lips.

But Clay couldn't revel in his victory for long. Alayna appeared beside him. "Good work. But let's get outside and keep watch, all right? I have a bad feeling." Her eyes searched his face.

Clay and Alayna marched through the church's double doors, waving to both Maia and Valerie as they headed for home. "Meet you there?" Valerie mouthed. And Clay nodded, knowing he'd find a way. He always did.

The rising glow of the moon faintly lit Main Street, giving it an ominous feeling. Clay moistened his chapped lips and felt a sudden stab of pain in his left forearm, where the lesion was. He presumed it had begun to blister. "Shit," he muttered.

"What is it?" Alayna asked. She looked harried, a

bit panicked. Her tight, black bun had nearly wound down her back, but she didn't notice it. She was rarely this unkempt.

But Clay didn't yet want to reveal his sores. "Just this day. Something about it doesn't add up for me," he muttered, watching as a family of three across the street began to load food items into the back of their van. A young girl of about six or seven held three cans of beans and peered out over the horizon, her eyes like saucers.

"You questioning things again?" Alayna asked him. "You know you don't have to think about everything all of the time. The world's evils are not always just around the corner."

Clay rubbed the back of his sweating neck as the girl thrust the cans of beans into the van before darting back into the house. "I suppose it's just my nature. I can't explain it. I have this gut feeling about today. It's ominous, certainly. But I can't help but feel like we don't have all the answers."

"Now who's been watching too many sci-fi movies?" Alayna said, laughing.

But Clay didn't react. Instead, his stomach throttled with sudden pain. He wrapped his hand over his abdomen, gasping. Alayna placed a steady hand on his lower back, sensing something was off.

"Dude, you're sweating. Like, a lot," she whispered. Her eyes scanned the street, ensuring no one else was noticing.

"The last thing I need right now is for Colonel Wallace to see me like this," Clay muttered. He righted himself as the spasm passed.

"You should really talk to the doc," Alayna pleaded. Everything about her was suddenly angular, panicked. Clay knew that if he agreed, she'd have no one left. And she couldn't monitor this town's evacuation by herself.

"The last thing I need right now is to be in some quarantine tent," Clay muttered, resting a loose hand on his gun. "Really, Alayna, I'm fine. It's probably just stress." He gave her a slight smile before asking, "So, how 'bout my speech in there? Seems I'm a real crowd pleaser, huh?"

Alayna rolled her eyes but still maintained her upset disposition. "You killed it. But it'll be all wasted breath if you're dead. You really need—"

Clay held his hand up, stopping Alayna's plea midsentence. "I'll take it easy, all right? If things advance, I'll talk to him at first chance. But for now, we need to be actively visible for the town's residents. Agreed?"

Alayna nodded but continued to wear her look of disagreement.

Clay forced himself to retain his composure. He and Alayna took turns marching down Main Street, watching as people packed their vans and cars, kissed their children, and sobbed openly, knowing that their lives were about to change. He stopped in front of a teenage boy who kicked his foot against a post. "Aren't you getting ready to go?" Clay asked him, tilting his head.

The teenage boy kicked the post harder, filled with anxiety. "Caleb was my best friend," he said. "If he's dead, we're all going to die. He was the best person I knew."

The boy's words, despite their melodramatic tone, impacted Clay, causing his chest to tighten. "Losing Caleb was a tragedy. But if you don't speed up and get out of here, your entire future, along with the future of your family, could be in jeopardy."

The boy's eyes gleamed with tears. His cheekbones were high, stark, without the baby face of his youth. "Fuck this, man," he said. "Seriously."

Clay's stomach lurched. He agreed wholeheartedly. But he pointed toward the boy's mother, who carried a large suitcase in her arms, stumbling wildly. "Just do the right thing. We all have to," he whispered.

Clay met Alayna back in front of the church, feeling the chill overtake the air as the moon rose farther above the horizon. The streetlamps buzzed, providing small strings of light at several different points for about a mile. Alayna shivered, rubbing at her upper arms. "I used to think this town was so cozy," she breathed. "Now, I've never been more frightened."

That's when they heard the first scream.

22.

Clay turned his head toward it, reaching for his gun. He saw a group of about ten people staggering toward them. When they drew close enough, their eyes flashed yellow beneath the streetlights. Their angry howls echoed against the old brick buildings. Clay rushed into the street, screaming for Alayna.

"They're infected! Get your gun!"

"We can't hurt them!" Alayna cried. "We know them!"

And sure enough, they did. Several of the crazed people coming toward them, staggering, bleeding purple blood from lesions on their heads and necks, had been the very people in the church's town meeting. They'd gazed up at Clay with wide eyes, taking his word as gospel. And then they'd rushed to their homes, eager to evacuate.

But it had been too late. They'd already turned.

Women ripped their nails over their blouses, causing blood to spurt from their breasts. Three children, all around the age of ten, flung themselves to the ground and began thrashing wildly, screaming. It looked like they were being exorcized. The feverish mob drew closer still to Clay and Alayna, their arms outstretched, their hair falling in clumps around them, leaving a trail.

“Shit. What are we going to do?” Alayna whispered. “We can’t take them all to quarantine. They’ll destroy us.”

Clay lifted his gun. It shook in the air as he aimed it toward the first man: the aging science teacher from the local high school. His mouth lolled open, and he lurched toward Clay, sending his erratic, bleeding arms toward Clay’s throat. He was screaming, his tongue lolling from his mouth.

As his fingers waved inches from Clay’s neck, Colonel Wallace’s soldiers appeared from around the corner and flung up their automatic weapons, shooting several holes through the science teacher’s stomach, dropping him to the ground. His limbs flailed. Beside Clay, Alayna screamed. But the noise was soon obliterated by the sound of countless automatic bullets pummeling through the crazed group, pounding them to the ground. Blood splattered violently across the church.

The silence after the shooting was deafening. Clay still held his gun elevated as the smoke cleared, revealing the sprawling bodies. Elbows pointed all direction. Their faces remained intact, blissful, almost angelic, if not for the few with bright and dripping legions.

“WHAT THE FUCK!” The teenage boy across the street, the one who’d been Caleb’s best friend, began to panic, waving his arms in a crazed way. But he didn’t have the virus. His fear was honest—the same fear that ravaged Clay’s heart.

But as the smoke cleared and the teenager continued his rambling, several of the dead men and women began to uncoil themselves from the ground. Miraculously, they pounded their hands upon the cement, lifting their elbows and upper bodies. They grinned ominously at Clay, their faces partially smashed in from the cement. And then they righted themselves on spindly, bullet-riddled legs and began their march toward him once more, their eyes still yellow, searching for him.

Clay stepped forward, confident. On instinct, he thrust his gun toward the heads of each of the men and women, shooting holes into their skulls. They flung back upon the ground, the brains spilling out behind their heads like a pillow. He shot them all—*bang, bang, bang*—the noise ringing through his ears.

And then, all at once, it was quiet. It was finished. Clay dropped his arm to his side, gasping. The silence around him was echoing, never ending. He collapsed upon his knees in immediate exhaustion. The facts of the day pounded into him: he'd killed nearly a dozen people, including Cliff, with a bullet to the brain.

The world was spinning.

He felt Wallace's presence beside him. He craned his neck, peering up, and felt the sweat dripping down his cheeks.

Wallace's voice pounded like the voice of God. "If you would have let me evacuate this place sooner, those lives wouldn't have been lost," he said. He gave Clay a look of extreme disappointment. "You better hope we can save the others."

Wallace strutted back toward his vehicle, leaving Clay to stare down at his hands. He felt oddly defeated. Alayna moved toward him, tapping his back, silently supporting him.

Clay lowered his head, turning the events of the day over in his mind. He swiped at the never-ending stream of perspiration, unable to draw the link between the meteorite and the sweat and—all of this.

His voice came in staggering bursts. "What the fuck is really going on here, Alayna?"

Before him, the people he was meant to save dribbled dry, their blood and guts pushing out over the cement. Alayna had no answer.

23.

Clay and Alayna staggered into the church, Clay gasping for air. He pounded his fist against the wall. His eyes darted back toward the open doors, noting that the evacuation had continued and that Colonel Wallace's men were already taking care of the dead bodies.

"Listen, Alayna. I want to make sure my family's all right," he said. He brushed his hand through his hair, feeling the strands release once more. "Would it be okay if I left you to handle things for a while? I'll be back as soon as I can. And then, you can go check on—"

Alayna nodded. "Actually, Megan's already left. She sent me a text that she'll meet me in Austin. We've been talking about going there for months now." She gave a small shrug. "Maybe the breakup's not quite so official, huh?"

Clay nodded, remembering that Alayna and her girlfriend, Megan, had been on the rocks in the previous few weeks. He'd given her the best advice he could, given that he'd never been a thirty-year-old bisexual woman. He tapped Alayna's shoulder, lightly kissed her cheek, and then rushed out to his sheriff's car, parked near the station.

"Hurry back!" Alayna called to him. Her voice echoed against the main street buildings. It chilled

Clay to the bone. But he reached his hand in the air and waved to her. He hoped that was assurance enough.

He sped toward home, winding down the back roads, taking the same route he had that morning. He blew through stop signs and stoplights, pushing past twenty miles per hour over the speed limit. When he was only two minutes from home, he felt he was going to jump out of his skin with anticipation. He just wanted to wrap his arms around his wife.

He burst into the house to find Valerie poised over a suitcase, stacking her mother's silver cutlery in the sides. She blinked at him brightly and then rushed toward him, wrapping him in a sure, cozy hug. She kissed his cheek. "Darling, you don't look well. Are you feeling all right? Can I make you some tea? I know you probably didn't eat enough today . . ." She trailed off, wandering to the kitchen.

Clay followed her, falling into the comfort of home. He heard Maia's music upstairs blaring. "Is she packing?" he asked. His voice was quieter than it had been the entire day. He didn't want to hear himself any longer.

"She is," Valerie said. "And pretty glad to be getting out of school for a while, frankly," she teased.

"Well, wouldn't we all be?" Clay said. He eyed the suitcase in the foyer. "You know, we should only be taking things that we absolutely need for the next month. Not china. Not cutlery. We can eat off paper plates if need be. Once we get to where we're going."

"And where in the world is that, exactly?" Valerie asked. She gave away her fear with a bright flash of her eyes. "This is all happening too damned fast, Clay." She eased into the chair across from him and dropped her face into her hands. "I can't remember ever feeling so frightened."

Clay brought his hand over her knuckles, kneading at them. "Listen, baby. We're going to get through this," he said. He felt slight anger riding within him—anger that she couldn't possibly understand how dire things really were. But he had to have strength for her.

"We'll meet in Austin," he offered, reminded of the place Alayna had said she and Megan would be. "I hear it's a beautiful place. We can treat it like a vacation. You know, you've been asking me to take a vacation for something like two years."

Valerie laughed through tears. She pulled her long fingers across her cheek, trying to orient herself. "Okay. Just the simple things, then," she said, shuddering. "Clothes. A bit of food for the journey."

"Right. And Maia, of course."

"Oh, shoot. I wanted to leave her behind," Valerie giggled.

For a moment, as they exchanged a smile, Clay could feel the passion he'd once had for this woman, back when they'd been high school sweethearts, making out in the back seat of his car. He'd felt assured in his belief that he never wanted to spend a day without her. And here he was, sending her away.

"I just want you two out of town, before anything . . . happens," Clay muttered, trailing off.

"Before what happens?" Valerie asked, frowning. "They're just going to fumigate, right? Everything will be right as rain again in a month. Right?"

"Sure," Clay said, nodding. An image of the crazed zombies swam through his mind once more. In an instant, he could imagine his wife into that role: the lesions dripping blood down her cheeks, her eyes yellow and manic. He quickly slammed the door on those horrific thoughts.

"Listen, Val," he said, kissing her hand. "Just get packed up and get going, okay? The sooner you leave, the better it will be. We just want to stay on top of this situation. No lollygagging. And watch your back out there, all right?"

Valerie nodded, parting her lips. She lifted her mouth over his and kissed him passionately. He could feel her hot tears rolling down her cheeks. He felt shattered, like shoving her away was a mistake he would regret. He wrapped his arms around her, yearning to crawl in bed with her, to forget the world.

But there wasn't time. The world was at their doorstep. And it wanted blood.

Over the next several hours, Clay helped his wife and daughter load up the SUV, ultimately insisting that they didn't pack the television, the china, or Maia's stuffed animal collection from when she was a little girl. "Just one," Clay insisted, not wanting to admit that he sort of loved that Maia was devolving in age as she acknowledged her fear. She wrapped her arms around him and sobbed for several moments, completely eliminating the wretched teenage persona he'd grown accustomed to. She was his little girl again.

Finally, about an hour before sunrise, Clay stood in the driveway as the SUV backed from the driveway. He gave them an earnest wave and smile even as his stomach began to lurch, even as the lesions on his forearm began dripping. With the last glimpse of his daughter's face vanishing, he suddenly realized he might never see her again.

He might never teach her to drive a car. Or walk her down the aisle for whatever bozo she married. Or watch her make a million and a half little mistakes, all of which didn't make a hill of beans compared to how much he loved her.

That was nonsense. Why would he think that? Of course he'd see her again. It was just a simple evacuation. Nothing more.

He couldn't understand these emotions. And, of course, he couldn't dwell on them. He stumbled into the house, feeling, at first, that he might vomit. But the purge didn't come. He tousled his hair, still noting that it was thinning. But he was feeling strangely better physically. He'd taken his wife and daughter and pushed them toward safety. And that made up for the rest of his ailments.

24.

Clay took a brief, five-minute shower, and scrubbed at his skin, breeding life back into his pulsing veins. He dressed quickly, his brain already humming with thoughts of Alayna. He hadn't heard from her since he'd left her late the night before, and he'd begun to imagine the worst.

He grabbed a last piece of bread and cheese, envisioning the soon-to-be-abandoned grocery store. Flies would flood the dairy section; all bread would mold. He shivered.

He dashed through town, his eyes tracing the horizon. The road that led toward the highway held a single line of cars, like ants, that stretched back toward the town square. The rising sun glinted against his wife's SUV, which was now toward the front, headfirst toward safety.

He parked the car on the deserted Main Street and walked with a bit of swagger toward the church, where he found Alayna leaning on the doorway, gazing out at the empty scene. The moment she saw him, all tension released in her face. "Damn it. You're finally here," she whispered, tossing her arms around him. She was quivering.

"What happened?" Clay asked, breaking their hug and searching her face. "Did more people turn into those crazed—"

Alayna shook her head. “Just the families. The mothers. They were crying so much, demanding answers from me. They told me that if it was up to me to save the town, they were sure they could never come back. It was horrible. These people, they’re running out of hope.”

“Don’t let them get to you, Alayna,” Clay said, his voice gruff. “When people are afraid, they say foolish, terrible things. You know this from the arrests you’ve made. How many times has Trudy told you you’re going to die alone?”

Alayna shrugged, her gaze looking somber and faraway. “She’s probably right.”

“Don’t be foolish. Megan will be waiting for you,” Clay said, despite having been a soft shoulder to cry on far too many times through her and Megan’s wildly intermittent relationship. “You’ll see. Now, let’s get this evacuation wrapped up and be on our way. I don’t want to stick around here any longer than we have to.”

As if on cue, Colonel Wallace barreled around the side of the church, assessing them with his mechanical eyes. “Sheriff,” he boomed. “It seems we’re nearly finished with the evacuation. I have to admit, I had my doubts allowing your method to proceed. But we’re ahead of my anticipated schedule. However, as you know, we have to complete this sweep with the utmost urgency. I’d like to introduce you to Lieutenant Adam Daniels. He’ll be the leader of the final steps of the evacuation.”

Clay took a step forward, trying to make eye contact with the lieutenant. His glassy eyes were bright blue and glared out across Main Street with a fierceness that caused Clay to think, beyond anything, that this man was crazy.

"Welcome to the team," Clay said. He kept his hands on his hips, unwilling to shake the man's hand.

Dr. Willis Miller appeared beside Clay then, becoming a welcome distraction from the cold, dead eyes of Lieutenant Daniels. "Sheriff, I've volunteered to stay behind to help with the evacuation. You never know when medical help might be needed," Willis said. The man was in his midthirties, a newcomer to the town. He'd moved his wife and two young sons there to take over the past pediatrician's position. Maia had seen him for her strep throat just a few months before.

"Thank you, Doctor," Clay offered, grateful to speak normally, without putting on any show for the colonel's sake. "Your wife and kids make it out okay?"

"Sent them to Alabama to be with their grandmother," Willis affirmed, his face looking grey. "I was around during the attack downtown earlier. I haven't seen humans act like that in all my years. Some kind of plague, possibly."

Clay cinched his lips together for a moment, fear rushing through him. If a doctor hadn't recognized that mania, then did they really have a chance? But he answered with confidence. "It's good we got the people out when we did."

A black town car began to rush down Main Street then. Clay brought his hand to his gun unconsciously and tried to peer into the dark glass, his heart pumping.

25.

Suddenly, the unfamiliar vehicle screeched to a halt and the back door swung open. Mayor Washington stepped out wearing a prim business suit, her hair swept back without a strand out of place. She sniffed, eyeing the empty town.

"Sheriff. Wonderful to see the process has been moving along smoothly," she said.

Except for the multiple bodies, Clay wanted to shout. The nightmare was rattling him. "We should be getting out soon, as well, Mayor," he said, still peering at Lois's unexpected transport.

Lois brought her hands together. "Yes. I think the plan will do well. Colonel Wallace and I will leave the four of you—our trusted doctor, the lieutenant, and of course our town sheriff and deputy—to it. You'll become responsible for the task of making a final sweep of the town." She snuck a peek at her slim watch, her face looking rodent-like. "After this moment, I believe, you'll have a little more than forty-eight hours to evacuate yourselves. After that, there's no guarantee that you'll be safe. Is that correct, Colonel?" Her eyes swept toward the colonel, who was standing on the other side of Lieutenant Daniels.

"Absolutely, ma'am," he affirmed. "We've established an energy field around the perimeter of the town. This 'containment zone' was put in place for safety reasons. We don't want whatever is circulating through the town to make it out. The fumigation, which will wipe out this virus, could be quite deadly to humans as well. It's set to go off at high noon in two days. Know that you'll all live a whole lot longer if you don't stick around for it to go off. Don't go getting curious on us." He flashed a daring smile toward Clay. "After you pass through the perimeter, you'll be placed in quarantine for safety reasons as well, but it should only be a temporary stay."

Clay stared sternly into the colonel's eyes. He felt the pangs of his ever-present gut-feeling rattle deep within. He knew something was off, but he wasn't exactly qualified to question all the specifics. He had to trust Lois's words earlier that she would explain everything at some point. She had been their faithful leader for far too long to begin questioning her now.

With an all too familiar motion, the colonel guided the mayor toward her waiting driver. "I hope I wasn't too pretentious ordering you the chauffeured car, Mayor," he said as he turned his back to the four remaining guardians. An unheard exchange passed between the two before he retreated to his revving military vehicle on the other side of the church.

"We'll see you all when this blows over," he called, as if he were speaking about a winter storm or a spat.

As the military transport zoomed down Main Street to join the line of cars that still chugged toward the highway, the four remaining members of Carterville joined in a small circle, eyeing each other ominously. Clay still sensed that Alayna was quivering, but her eyes looked sharp; her mind was clear. When the ship began to sink, he wanted to be in her lifeboat.

"I'd like to thank all of you for staying," Clay said, searching the glassy-eyed face of Lieutenant Daniels and the bearded, soft, folding face of Doctor Miller. A wind kicked up, whooshing against the doctor's flannel, causing him to wrap it tighter around his thin frame. "We're going to figure this out," Clay continued, his own voice doubtful. "And if we don't, at least we'll ensure no more people die today. Is that clear?"

No one responded. Silence seemed to creep around them, filling the air with tension. The town was turning grey and blank.

26.

The four stood near the church, the wind continuing to whip around them, as Clay and Alayna began to cook up a plan to organize their next two days. They peered at a map stretched out between them, orchestrating sections for each of them to search.

"Willis, you think you could head to the neighborhood near the high school?" Alayna asked. "I know we had a few stragglers there a few hours ago."

"Not a problem," Willis affirmed.

Clay handed him a walkie-talkie. "As you recall, there's no cell service, thanks to the military," Clay said with a quick glance at Daniels. "And we'll need these to keep in touch when we're separated." Clay continued to hand radios to the Alayna and Daniels.

Willis grasped the radio with thick fingers, his eyes toward the ground. "I hope they make it to Alabama," he whispered, lost in the emotions of saying good-bye. Beside him, Daniels snorted, rolling his eyes. All sense of compassion was lost. But, to be fair, Clay knew they didn't have time for it.

Alayna blinked rapidly, eyeing the few downtown streets. She rubbed at her temple. A single blue vein stuck out from her skin, giving her a ghoulish look. "It's so goddamn quiet," she said. "I've never seen it like this."

Clay felt his gut churning again. Everything about the world seemed to tilt; the air tasted wrong. He knew that Alayna was saying the obvious, sure. But there was something more to this feeling—something that assured him that everything wasn't precisely as it seemed. Colonel Wallace and the mayor had seemed so chummy, too familiar together. Almost as if—

His mind couldn't articulate just how wrong this feeling was. He shook his head and muttered under his breath, allowing only Alayna to hear. "Something's not right. It's . . . it's just a feeling."

Alayna turned toward him, placing a firm hand upon his shoulder. "You have to stop with the 'gut feeling' bullshit, Clay. I know you're my boss and all, but it's creeping me out. You've told me before. We have to look at the facts of a given situation. And we have to focus on those facts. And the fact is, we need to get moving."

"But doesn't it seem odd to you that less than forty-eight hours ago, the town was running along just fine? Then, out of nowhere, a meteorite blasts through the night and interrupts life as we know it. Don't you think a complete town evacuation seems a bit overkill, and in such haste? And how did the military know about everything so soon?" Clay paused to study the blank stares from everyone around him. Everyone except Lieutenant Daniels. His stare reeked of boredom. "They were already on their way before news of the catastrophe even made it out of town, almost as if they were on their way here for some other reason altogether."

The foursome remained silent for several moments, each of their minds turning over the words

Clay had just uttered.

Suddenly, a gale-force wind nearly knocked them over before it ripped the town map from their grasp. They tried to recapture the map, but the abrupt blast of cool air had blown everyone's hair into their eyes, causing a momentary loss of clarity.

27.

Clay surprised everyone with his sudden catlike reflexes as he snatched the map out of the whirling gust. "I think we need to find a base of operations. The church is too barren and too strange. We'll need to find protection from the elements until we're ready to leave town."

"The station?" Willis asked.

"No. It's too far from the center of the containment zone, unfortunately," Clay said. He blinked several times and then pointed, slowly, toward the historic hotel on the corner. The Masonic Hotel on Main Street was painted a bright canary yellow, with large bay windows, giving it the appearance of a house on a Northeastern bay where he and his wife had stayed once. They'd left Maia at home with a babysitter and scouted out a brief night for themselves. Unfortunately, they'd both been so exhausted, they'd just fallen asleep in each other's arms, with a Lifetime movie blaring on the television. Such was marriage. Such was life.

"The hotel?" Alayna asked, biting her lip. "I suppose it's our best option right now."

"Damn right it is," Clay said, allowing certainty to fuel his words. "Plus, it gives us enough room to take turns getting some rest over the next three days. And I'm sure it's well stocked with food."

The four of them bounded toward the hotel, Alayna folding the map quickly and tucking it back in her pocket. They climbed up the porch, where four antique rocking chairs swayed in the wind, and then entered the empty foyer, looking around wide-eyed at the wonder that was a completely naked front desk, a clock that continued to tick without anyone to notice, and a phone that would sit unattended for at least thirty days.

"It hasn't been closed in over a hundred years," Alayna whispered, sliding her finger along the gleaming wood of the front desk. "And now, who knows when it'll open again."

As she spoke, Daniels swept past her quickly, nearly knocking her over. He quickly grabbed the map from her back pocket, his eyes flashing.

"Hey!" Alayna cried. The violation caused her to step back, reeling.

But Daniels had already splayed the map on the desk, stabbing his finger across the different areas. "Don't worry about it, little lady." He held her gaze for a moment before eyeing the rest of her taut body. "We need to get cracking. I've never seen such nostalgia in a group of rescuers. Out here, it's either fight for survival or be killed."

Willis's eyebrows rose high with immediate fear. Clay tapped his hand over his gun, sensing this man was a loose cannon. Why on earth had the colonel left him? And on top of that, it was clear he didn't mind being forceful and pushy with their only female attendant. His stomach tighten with anger.

But Daniels continued without pause. "We need to start from the outside and move inward, toward home base. We need to round up as many of the remaining locals as possible. We'll meet here after dark, maybe around nine, and put together a nourishing meal." He sniffed for a moment, turning his eyes toward Clay. "It's clear that some of us aren't ready to take charge of such a serious situation. Which is why I'm here."

Clay clenched his fists, anger throttling through him. But he swallowed, forcing himself to focus. They had to find the stragglers. They couldn't linger on small spats. And, despite finding a deep, impenetrable hatred for this man growing within him, he needed to look beyond it.

28.

Lieutenant Daniels traced out the blocks on the map methodically as the three others watched him, shifting their weight from foot to foot and feeling panic after each tick of the clock. Time was passing quickly, and the sun would dip beneath the horizon all too soon.

Finally, Daniels began to bark orders. "I think for safety reasons, we work in pairs," he said, daring anyone to interrupt him. "I'll work with the woman." His eyes crept back toward Alayna's body, easing over her curves.

To Clay, it was apparent that the attraction was purely one-sided. Although Alayna had dated both men and women, she'd been dating primarily the latter throughout her late twenties, due to her sheer distaste for men just like Daniels.

Alayna crossed her arms over her chest, almost physically hiding herself. Her eyes made momentary contact with Clay's, but she didn't show her annoyance or her fear. She knew the circumstances were far greater than that.

"I'll go with Willis, then," Clay said, eyeing the doorway. "But we need to get going."

"Follow the map I've drawn you," Daniels said, pointing. "You'll take the west side of town, near the high school. And the girl and I will take the east."

"The girl has a name," Clay said harshly, before abruptly turning from Daniels toward Willis, noting that he still held his walkie-talkie like a plaything. "You good, Doctor?"

"You should know that I don't know how to operate a weapon," Willis said, looking slightly defeated. "I can mend wounds and heal broken bones and give you penicillin, but I've never even held a gun."

"It's okay," Clay said, even as his heart palpitated. "That's not why you're here. You're here in case we come across anyone wounded or hurt. We'll take care of the rest."

Alayna nodded beside him, bringing her hand to the gun at her side. "Clay's got your back," she said. "We have enough guns and know-how between the rest of us to keep everyone safe until we get out of Dodge ourselves. I'm not worried. And you shouldn't be either."

Willis nodded, drumming his fingers over his sweating temple. "Sure. Okay. I'll have my medical pack, then. And if the two of you have any problems, you'll call me on this walkie-talkie, yeah?"

"Of course," Alayna said, her voice almost chipper. "This town isn't big enough for us to lose track of each other. We have vehicles. We can come together in ten or fifteen minutes if need be."

"Let's go," Daniels said then, bursting toward the door, his keys jangling at his side. "We need to move. Come on, Alayna."

Alayna tossed Clay a sober glare before following after, leaving Clay and Dr. Miller alone in the shadowed hotel foyer, the ancient floorboards creaking beneath them. Clay searched his pocket for his keys, thinking they'd drive out to the farthest point on their designated side of town, and was grateful they'd have a few hours away from that wretched man.

"Who does he think he is?" Willis asked as they walked toward Clay's patrol vehicle. "Such an asshole."

"Think of it like this: as soon as we evacuate ourselves, he won't be a part of our lives anymore," Clay said. "I guess when you're thrust into such an unpredictable situation, you can't always choose who you'll be surrounded by. Imagine if you were on the Titanic, sinking next to the most annoying guy in the world. It's completely out of your control."

Willis laughed appreciatively, clutching his medical pack firmly. He spat on the ground. "It's so creepy around here," he whispered. "Although I didn't grow up in Carterville, I wanted to raise my sons here. And now—"

"We're going to get it back," Clay affirmed, slipping into the driver's seat. Willis climbed in beside him without agreeing. "We're going to get it back," he said again, almost trying to convince himself in the midst of such desolation.

As they drove, Clay began to consider his symptoms: the hair falling out, the scabs and lesions on his arms and now his legs, and the vomiting. They seemed all too similar to the ones exhibited by Cliff what seemed like years ago. But perhaps, with the doctor's help, he could know for certain. Perhaps he'd diagnose him with a stress disorder. He'd tell him it was common that people exhibited these symptoms when they were frightened or fighting a battle they weren't sure they'd win. Hadn't he heard that people lost their hair from sadness or divorce or just moving across the country?

But he held his tongue, thinking he'd tell Willis about his symptoms after they'd cleared out a few houses and inched back toward home base. Plus, he was frightened at what the diagnosis might be. What if something was really wrong? What if he *was* going to turn into one of the crazed, biting and thrashing? He shuddered at the thought, spinning the tires as he picked up speed. Willis was stoic, sitting beside him, clearly filled with his own thoughts and fears.

29.

Lieutenant Daniels drove like a maniac to the outskirts of town, causing Alayna's head to buck up against the glass.

"Can you not do that?" she said under her breath, wishing she'd been paired with any other person. Daniels was clearly a mental case, a man who'd seen combat for too many years and no longer knew how to see the outside world. Everything was danger—immediate. And she—a woman—was just something to look at. It was infuriating.

"I think we should start with that group of houses over there," Alayna said, pointing toward the area where her mother's parents had lived so long before. "I know a lot of older people live there. Maybe they've been left behind or couldn't get out in time."

Daniels scoffed but spun the wheel toward the houses, stopping short at the side of the road. He tapped his gun and turned toward her. "So, you're sure you can protect yourself if we encounter any of those . . . crazies?"

"I think I can handle myself," Alayna said, keeping her eyes toward the houses, searching for signs of life.

"Because, you know, I've killed many men," Daniels said, clearly trying to flirt with her. "I can protect both of us if you want me to walk alongside you. I can even hold your hand if you get frightened."

Alayna couldn't believe what she was hearing. Her jaw dropped open. With a sudden movement, she flipped the door open and burst out, her focus on the business at hand. She heard Daniels's heavy footfalls behind her as she headed toward the houses, and she furrowed her eyebrows, attempting to look ugly, haggard, serious.

"You know, I think you're different than the other girls I've seen on forces across the country," Daniels said, taking an easy stride beside her. "You're definitely beautiful, for one. But you're tough. Resilient. Many women I know wouldn't have stayed behind like this, you know. You must have the kind of bravery I look for in a partner. In someone I could see myself with for good."

"Hmm?" Alayna asked, hardly listening. Her eyes traced the dark windows of the homes, looking for any sign of light. The sun was drifting through the sky, casting narrow shadows along the ground.

"That is, if you could handle someone like me," Daniels said, snorting slightly. "I only date if it's worth my time. And, having been in the service for so long, being out in the field, saving both this country and others around the world, it's a struggle to find women to suit my way of life."

"Is that so?" Alayna said, marching toward the front door of the first house, rapping her knuckles against the wood. "HELLO?" she called, her voice shaking slightly. She hoped Daniels wouldn't notice. She couldn't look weak in front of him.

"Anyway, when this all blows over," he continued, as they marched on to the next house, "I wouldn't mind seeing where we could go."

"What do you mean 'we'?" Alayna asked, pursing

her lips. She knocked on the next door, sensing no movement in the house. A neglected flowerbed sat beside the door, crackling and allowing the petals to fall. It saddened her and reminded her of another, better time: when the town had been flourishing. When they hadn't felt the very real presence of danger.

"We could see each other. We could be with each other. I think you'd be pretty impressed with how I handle a woman in the bedroom—" Daniels began, his voice booming.

Alayna spun toward him, this last comment violating her and causing her brain to burn. "Excuse me? You won't be handling this woman in the bedroom ever." She thought briefly of Megan, waiting for her in Austin. She yearned to wrap her arms around her, to kiss her. They'd struggled in the past, sure. But didn't all couples? Since their latest breakup, she'd eyed couples at restaurants, bickering, tossing nasty words at each other. She and Megan had been there before, and she always regretted it after each episode. Their love had been beaten down, but they always rebuilt it fresh each time. Now she could almost feel their love for one another stretch across time and space. She felt she could feel Megan thinking about her, all those miles away—assured she would make it out of the containment zone alive.

"Don't be so rash, baby," Daniels said, his voice dropping. "I could really be something for you. I could fulfill you in ways you couldn't have dreamed."

Alayna nearly spat in his face. "Listen here, Lieutenant. I wouldn't sleep with you if you were the last man on earth. And I mean that, one hundred percent." Her eyes flashed angrily. She stomped away from him and toward the last house on the block, her fists clenched after the intensity of her words.

But when she reached the red-painted doorway of this house, she was shocked to see that the door was popped open, and she heard a radio crackling inside. She felt Daniels's presence behind her as she pushed open the door, revealing the shadowed interior.

30.

Clay parked near a subdivision on the outskirts of town, gazing at the empty streets. Ordinarily, on a day like this, children would be cycling, people would be out walking their dogs, holding hands with their loved ones. But today, the garage doors were down, like closed mouths. Windows were latched.

"Let's just go one by one and knock on peoples' doors, I suppose," Clay said, shutting the car door with a bang that echoed across the emptiness. "Good to you?"

"Sure," Willis answered.

They walked together silently, down the center of the street, and then broke off evenly, Clay marching up to the three-story house on the corner and Willis taking the ranch home across the street. Clay banged on the door, gazing into the windows, seeing nothing but darkness. An empty dog food bowl outside alerted him: they'd left, and they'd obviously taken the dog with them. Good.

He continued, keeping tabs on Willis's trek on the other side of the street, his feet sinking into the perfectly mowed grass. He remembered when he was younger and had focused on the lawn a great deal more, ensuring that the weeds were eliminated, watching the way the mild green transformed into a rich, vibrant, almost rainforest green. Of course, when he'd taken the position of sheriff, he'd allowed the weeds to grow. He'd allowed the luster to diminish. The town become his yard. And he'd had to let some things go.

After the fifth house, Clay looked across the street to Willis. "Hey! You find anyone yet?" he asked, already knowing the answer.

"Nothing," Willis called back. "Seems like they're all gone."

"Good!" Clay said. "Let's head back to the car and move on."

Willis began to drift from the front door of a two-story home, his head down, watching his steps. Clay was walking toward him when he noticed something moving behind the home's big picture window.

"Willis!" Clay cried. "I think there's someone—"

But before he could finish, a figure came crashing through the glass, screaming. The man, someone Clay recognized as his daughter's second-grade baseball coach, lurched toward them, his eyes crazed, his skin almost green with illness. Scabs and lesions caked his arms and shoulders and neck, oozing blood and pus. Behind him, two teenage girls came crawling out, screaming and stabbing their fingers on the bits of leftover glass. They were converging on Willis, who had reached for his walkie-talkie, looking immediately defeated, like a drowning victim giving up on his lashing.

"WILLIS!" Clay cried, running toward him and the crazed monsters. He drew his gun and began to shoot, panic driving his trigger finger. A single bullet blasted through one of the girl's shoulders, painting gore on the side of the house. She was hardly bothered and continued to stagger forward.

Willis lurched back, but he wasn't quick enough.

The man brought his hands around Willis's neck and then bared his teeth, tearing a bit of flesh from Willis's shoulder. Willis let out a throaty scream. The sound rattled the windows and echoed through the barren street. He whipped back from the crazed, monstrous being just in time for Clay to push around him and plant a bullet directly in the monster's head. The father of two, the ex-baseball coach, flung back on the perfect grass, sanguine fluid seeping from his brain.

On instinct, Clay turned and shot both girls in the forehead. They fell back, leaving him and Willis in complete silence, hearing only their own gasps of panic.

"Shit," Clay whispered. "I thought we were in the clear. I thought we were okay."

Willis turned his chin toward his shoulder, tapping at the wound. Blood oozed down his chest, painting his shirt. "I need to get my medical pack," he whispered. "Jesus, this is deep."

Clay ran back to his cruiser and grabbed the pack, opening it quickly and eyeing the gleaming tools, the thread and scissors, the bandages. "What do you need?" he asked, still gasping.

Using his good hand, Willis riffled through the bag, finding alcohol, ointment, and a massive bandage. He dropped to the ground, tearing his sleeve away from his body and tossing the blood-soaked cloth away. He began to douse the wound with alcohol, wincing as he did.

Clay stood beside him, hand upon his gun, his eyes searching the horizon. The very moment he'd assumed they were safe, it had become apparent that nothing—not this cardboard subdivision, not a seemingly empty afternoon—was safe any longer. He couldn't let his guard down like that.

As he stood, the three dead crazed—three in a count of how many now—oozed dry beside him. His heart lurched with panic and pain. Just like the hairs on his head, he felt his inner sanity slip away, strand by strand.

31.

"Hello?" Alayna called. She searched the foyer and the living room without catching sight of a single figure. "Is anyone there?"

The radio was blasting out from the back part of the house. Alayna brought her hand to her gun, remembering the mania of the crazed, the way their brains had oozed out over the pavement. "I'm coming in!" she called. "Don't make any sudden movements!" These were words she hadn't spoken before—words that were reminiscent of a cop show she'd watched on television while growing up, dreaming of a better life.

"I don't think anyone's here," Daniels said, his voice booming.

Suddenly, a woman appeared before them. She was thin, frail, her white hair like a halo around her head. Her eyes flashed with anger. She clutched a cast iron skillet and waved it through the air, almost on time with the '50s radio station.

"What the fuck are you doing in my house?" the woman rasped. "Get out, you fools. Get out!"

Alayna recognized the woman but couldn't place her name. She held up her hands. "I'm sorry, ma'am. We're here to evacuate the entire town. We wanted to make sure everyone was aware."

"Well, I'm not leaving," the woman said, scowling.

"I've lived in this house for twenty-five years, and I'm not leaving it for some government takeover. Believe me, it's not worth it." She sniffed. "My Hector built me this house. And now he's gone, and it's all I've got, damn it."

Alayna took an additional step back, her boot squeaking on the linoleum. "I understand, ma'am. But know that nobody's going to take over your house. If you stay here, you could die. We're only evacuating everyone for the next thirty days. And then you can come back. You can have your life again." She swallowed. "Please know that I can't leave you here. It's best if you come with us, now."

The woman continued to glare, but she couldn't find words. Her skillet dropped a bit in the air. She was losing steam.

"What's your name, ma'am?" Alayna asked, noting that the woman didn't appear ill. She didn't exhibit any of the symptoms of the previously exposed. Not a single bit of sweat glossed over her forehead.

"I'm Norah," the woman spat. "Who's the asshole you brought in here?"

Alayna had to suppress the urge to laugh. "That's Lieutenant Adam Daniels," she said.

"Hello, ma'am," Daniels said, standing beside Alayna, his gun in his hand, pointed toward the ground. "We have to get you out of here." His words were insistent.

"He seems horrible," Norah said, rolling her eyes. She dropped the skillet on the countertop beside her, gesturing for Alayna to come closer. Alayna stepped into the kitchen, listening to the swell of oldies music, and noting that the woman had been eating a can of soup with a spoon. The room seemed lonely and sad, and yet it was clean, glowing with Norah's apparent scrubbing.

"It's a beautiful house," Alayna offered.

"Like I said, he built it," Norah said, collapsing into a chair at the kitchen table. "And it's all I have."

"Norah," Alayna whispered, knowing they were running out of time, "I was wondering if you would come with me, just for tonight. We can put you up in the hotel on Main Street until we can figure out where to send you, just until this all blows over. Do you have family somewhere?"

"I have a daughter in Charleston," the woman said. "But she never calls."

"Do you have her number?" Alayna asked.

"Of course I have her number," Norah snapped. "She's my daughter. Why wouldn't I have it?"

Alayna heard Daniels sigh behind her. She was conscious of his eyes on her backside, on her naked neck.

"It's okay, Norah," Alayna said. "We're going to get you there, no trouble. And then we'll get you back to this house when they give us the all clear."

"And you won't take anything?" Norah asked.

"Not a thing. I promise. Nobody is going to break into your house. Nobody will have any reason to at all," Alayna affirmed. "You're just going to have to trust me on this one."

Norah rose from the chair onto quivering knees. She glared back toward Daniels, clearly upset with his presence. "I'll go with you. I wondered what the heck happened to everyone," she murmured. "Although, I did see my neighbor Carl just this morning." Her eyebrows furrowed. "He seemed strange. Off."

32.

After the doctor patched himself up, strapping the bandage across his shoulder, Clay helped him back to the passenger seat, noting that the doctor was breathing heavily and still visibly frightened.

"Shit, man. I'm so sorry," Clay offered, unsure of what to say. He was rattled himself—not because of the killing but because it didn't bother him. He eyed the doctor as he cranked up the engine. "How's your pain?"

"It's not bad," the doctor said gruffly.

Clay hesitated. "I'm wondering if maybe we should get you back to the hotel and renew the search in the morning."

Willis shook his head. "If it's all the same, I think we should keep going. All I'd do back at the hotel is writhe in self-pity and think about allowing myself to get bitten," he said with despair. "Really. I can manage."

"Maybe just a few more neighborhoods, then," Clay said, still uncertain. "I should have been quicker with my gun."

"Don't worry about it. God knows I put enough antiseptic on this thing to kill off the bubonic plague," he joked.

Clay steered the car toward the next neighborhood, his anxiety and panic high. He parked in front of a group of homes, noting that the doctor's bandage had already begun to bleed through. "Maybe you should patch that up again. I'll check out the houses. You stay here."

The doctor agreed, sighing slightly and allowing his head to droop forward. Clay noted that the doctor had begun to sweat, albeit lightly. He hoped this was simply a result of the increased anxiety rather than one of Clay's own symptoms.

"Okay. I'll be right back," Clay affirmed, bolting from the car and sprinting toward the houses. He rapped on several doors without answer. He'd begun to feel that everyone had abandoned their homes and followed their instructions, that this was a waste of time. He could be far away, heading toward Austin—toward his wife and daughter—ready to take a much-needed break from these treacherous events. In a few years, this would seem like a dream.

The final house on the block had a single light blaring in the back room. Anxious, Clay knocked on the door loudly, calling out. "Hello? Is there someone there?" He turned back, eyeing his cruiser, noting that the doctor had leaned his head against the window and closed his eyes.

Moments later, the light snapped off. Clay lifted his gun from his holster, uneasiness passing through him. "HELLO?" he cried again, knocking once more. He took several steps back, then pummeled his body into the wood, feeling the door creak. "I'm going to shoot through your windows if you don't let me in!" he called again. Whoever it was, he needed to get them out. Immediately. He wouldn't be responsible for a meaningless death.

Finally, he heard someone behind the door, unlocking the bolt. A small face appeared in the crack, looking at him with big, hopeful eyes. Immediately, Clay recognized the woman. He nearly dropped his gun with surprise.

33.

Alayna's heartbeat surged. "What do you mean 'off'?" she asked.

"He was marching half-naked through my backyard, drooling all over himself. I mean, the man's almost seventy-five, sure. But he should know how to control himself."

"Do you know where he went?" Alayna asked, realizing that this man, Carl, had become one of them—one of the crazed—he'd turned..

"God only knows," Norah said. "Let me pack a few things. Then I'll go with you. And you"—she snapped at Daniels—"don't you stay in here. Go outside."

Daniels turned toward Alayna, looking for affirmation. Was this really happening? But Alayna shooed him, shoving him toward the door. "Just keep a lookout for Carl. He's most likely infected."

Alayna waited for Norah to finish packing, watching her drift through her downstairs, slide fingers over little knickknacks and portraits of her and her husband, probably photographed forty years before. Alayna recognized the love between them. She wondered if she and Megan could ever have that kind of love. The love that would last decades, even into death. Deep down, she knew she had it in her, but Megan was so unreadable sometimes. It made her crazy, and perhaps that is why she stayed.

As she stood, she heard several blasts from a gun outside. Above her, Norah began to scream in her bedroom. Panicked, Alayna rushed upstairs to find her gazing out the window at the sidewalk below. She heaved with terror.

"That monster," she breathed. "He killed Carl."

Outside, Daniels stood with his gun still poised, staring down at Carl splayed upon the cement. His arms and legs were flung out, and his blood began to leak from his ear and the back of his head. His reading glasses were still perched on his face.

"It's okay," Alayna whispered. "Carl was no longer the man you knew. He was coming to kill you. He was sick." She rubbed the old woman's back, feeling the spindly bones.

"Great. Now your lieutenant friend will kill us next," Norah said curtly.

"Why would you think that, Norah?" Alayna asked. Her own reservations about Daniels were triggered by his chauvinistic tendencies, not because he was a manic killer.

"Listen, I've been around long enough to know when I see a bad seed. That man is . . . is . . . he's just bad news."

Alayna smiled. "He certainly is rigid, but I have to believe it's just his training that's made him that way," she said, hoping she was right. Having only recently met him, and having endured his despicable flirting, she despised having to defend him.

Norah turned back toward her suitcase and zipped it, her eyebrows furrowed. "All right. If we're going to go, then I'd like to do it now or never. Thank you."

Alayna nodded, noting the time. The sun blasted

orange across the many houses, making them look forsaken, somehow.

34.

"Megan?" Clay said, in complete surprise.

"Hey, Sheriff," she said sheepishly, sweeping her dark bangs from her eyes. "Sorry about the door. And the light. I just—I didn't want to be found. But . . . here you are."

"Megan, you aren't supposed to be here," Clay said, feeling the all too familiar pangs of agitation for Alayna's on-again, off-again mate. "Alayna said you'd already left for Austin. I sent my family that way as well. We were all going to meet you there."

Megan bit her lip, allowing an awkward silence to pass as the door creaked open a bit wider. She motioned Clay into the foyer.

"Did you forget something?" Clay asked.

"No. I mean, kind of," Megan whispered, her voice cracking.

"Then what?" Clay asked, incredulous. Once again Megan was making bad decisions. She had to understand the importance and terror of what they were dealing with, almost more than anyone because of her relationship with Alayna.

"You know Al and I have had our troubles, right?" Megan asked, her voice wistful. "I'm sure she's told you, at least a little. The two of you are close. I think she looks at you as more than just a boss."

Clay nodded slowly, sensing the passage of time. They were wasting it.

"I told Alayna I wouldn't allow us to be split up again. When she sent me to Austin, I started out of town but then turned back. I knew I couldn't leave her here. Not alone." She brought her lips together, allowing the silence to stretch on. "Besides, Alayna told me everything was going to be fine eventually. So I saw no reason to be so far away from her."

Clay's eyes grew wide. "Sure, it's going to be okay—eventually. But not for a long while," he said, bringing a firm hand to her shoulder. "Listen, Megan. We need to get the hell out of here. They're fumigating in"—Clay paused to look at his watch—"well, in less than two days, and it'll most likely kill you. Do you understand?"

Megan's lip began to quiver with fear. "What—" she said, looking suddenly helpless. She was almost childlike compared to Alayna's loud, brilliant beauty.

"You need to come with us if you want to live, Megan," Clay said, his eyebrows furrowing. "I'm not fucking around. I'm not being dramatic. Alayna wasn't straight with you, and she should have been. But she just didn't want to scare you. Okay?"

Megan swallowed sharply, cutting back toward the side of the house and gripping her backpack, which was still packed from her previous attempt to leave. She sighed heavily and flung it around her shoulders, easing her feet into her tennis shoes. "You don't have any food, do you?" she asked, her voice high-pitched. "I'm starving."

"We can get something when we get back to the hotel," Clay said, finding the first grin in a while stretch across his face. Despite his frustration with Megan for coming back, it was good to feel that he'd actually done something positive during their search. He'd found someone; he'd convinced her to come to safety. All was not lost.

Megan sat in the back of the cruiser, her backpack on her lap, blinking wide doe eyes and not speaking as they drove closer to downtown. The doctor had begun to shiver, large beads of sweat on his forehead. Clay gripped the steering wheel with increasing intensity, punching his foot against the gas pedal. Houses whizzed past them.

At a stop sign, Clay paused, catching sight of a house with an upstairs light on. He stopped the vehicle and barreled up the steps of the house, rapping on the door, and collecting two more individuals. Ralph and Connie Sullivan were panicked, sure that staying was the "right thing to do." As he eased them into the back of his cruiser, his hands on their quivering backs, he assured them that everything would be fine. Safety was elsewhere. But they'd get Carterville back to normal soon, he promised. He lied.

35.

Clay parked alongside Lieutenant Daniels's military vehicle, noting that the hotel's lights were blaring, giving it an aura of warmth. He sighed with relief, listening as his two latest rescuees twittered with mild panic in the back seat. Clay remembered seeing the married couple many times at Sunday service, but he'd never interacted with them directly. It was clear now that they had an incredibly Christian background, bordering on the fanatical, as they prayed with manic zeal the moment they'd buckled in. Beside them, Megan rolled her eyes, gripping her backpack closer.

"Can you let us out of here?" Megan asked, bringing her lips together tightly. "I, for one, would like a bit of breathing room. And a bit less praying."

"Prayer is the only thing that will get us through this terrible time," Connie rasped. "You have to know that."

"Seriously, Clay. I can't open the back door myself. We're in a cop car, remember?" Megan said.

"Right," Clay said, rushing to open the door. Connie, Ralph, and Megan spilled out, stretching their limbs and backs and eyeing the warmth of the hotel. Willis took tentative steps from the vehicle, clearly weakened, fading with every moment.

"You gonna be okay, Doc?" Ralph asked with a

twang. "It looks like he's bleedin' bad."

Clay placed a hand at Willis's back, guiding him toward the door. "He'll be fine. We're all going to be fine," he said, feeling more and more unsure of whether those promises would hold up. Willis made momentary eye contact with him, looking like a tired, lost child and not like the emboldened doctor who'd volunteered to stay behind.

Clay opened the door to discover Daniels and Alayna standing at the foyer desk, their eyes upon the town map. Immediately, Alayna's face broke into a grin. She rushed toward Clay and wrapped her thin arms around his neck, shuddering. "I was so worried about you guys. Welcome back."

As she broke the hug, her eyes gazed over the people behind him, including the injured doctor, Ralph, Connie, and, of course, Megan. She took a tentative step back, bringing her fingers to her red-tinged cheek. "Megan? Wha . . . what are you doing here?" she gasped.

Megan stood in the doorway, allowing Ralph and Connie to skirt past her, muttering to themselves. It was unclear if their words were complaints or prayers.

"I was worried about you," Megan whispered. "I couldn't let you be here alone. I told you we wouldn't be without each other again. Not after our fight."

Alayna closed her eyes tightly. Crow's feet formed on either side, along with a small, intimate wrinkle between her eyebrows. "Damn it, Megan. You don't know what you've done." She flung herself forward, then, and kissed Megan fully, grasping her dark hair. A single tear swept down her cheek. "But it's so good to see you. I missed you."

"I missed you too," Megan said. She grinned,

similar tears showing in her eyes.

Near the formal dining room, Ralph and Connie glared at them, their jaws dropping. Clay was incredibly grateful that they didn't spout any of their biblical speak in that moment and simply allowed Megan and Alayna's beautiful embrace. Inwardly, he felt anxious and sad, wishing Valerie could be in his arms. As his mind wandered, he noticed Norah glaring at him.

"What are you looking at?" she asked.

Feeling slapped, Clay raised his hand in the air, ignoring the woman, and Megan and Alayna broke apart. "Everyone. I'd like to suggest that we regroup on the second floor to recap the events of today, make plans for tomorrow, and relax, above all. Get cleaned up if you like, and meet in the bar in thirty minutes. Meanwhile, I'll take a look at our food situation."

"I'll come too," Alayna said, leaving one last peck on Megan's cheek.

The group split up with somber looks, walking off to claim hotel rooms for themselves. The doctor moved with intent but struggled visibly. His feet paused at every other step, and his eyes narrowed with concern. Clay and Alayna watched him until he reached the landing, when Alayna whispered, "We really need to watch the doc. Is he going to be okay?"

"I think he'll be fine. He was bitten by one of the crazed but hasn't shown any signs of the infection. We talked earlier, and he says that he can treat himself. Seeing as nobody else in this group has any medical training, I think he's his own best option."

Alayna gave him a knowing glance. "Are you sure about that?"

"No. Of course not," Clay said, turning toward the kitchen. "But we have to be optimistic. I honestly don't know what to think anymore. But if he stayed behind to help medically, then he should be able to at least treat the bite himself. Don't you think?"

"Sure," Alayna whispered, trailing off.

36.

They popped open the kitchen door and found themselves in a gleaming aisle of stainless steel refrigerators and cabinets, all stocked with meats, cheeses, breads, vegetables, and fruits—enough to feed their small group for a week. They allowed themselves a few moments of play, nibbling on bits of cheese and creating a large tower of fruits, before carrying as much as they could to the second-floor bar. They splayed the foods upon the bar top and waited for the survivors to assemble.

Megan appeared in the doorway of the bar first, her freshly washed hair dribbling down her back. She grinned sheepishly at Alayna, who grasped her hand and squeezed it before dropping it away. "Have something to eat. You look hungry," she said.

Megan lifted an apple to her mouth and bit into it, creating that familiar crisp, fresh sound. Alayna held her gaze, leaving Clay to stuff his hands in his pockets and monitor the liquor cabinets. Eyeing the massive collection the hotel bartender, Harvey, had amassed through the years, Clay was generally impressed, even though his own knowledge of wine and spirits was limited.

Several minutes later, the entire group had arrived, poised and attentive. Clay placed his palms upon the mahogany bar top and assessed his random group, noting that the doctor was alert but his appearance had deteriorated even further in the short time since he'd last seen him.

"All right, guys," Clay began, clearing his throat. "I want to thank you all for your hard work today. Alayna and Lieutenant Daniels, I appreciate you bringing Norah in. And discovering Megan, Ralph, and Connie today was truly a blessing. We wouldn't have wanted them out there in this hell."

"Hear, hear," Alayna said, raising her fist. Daniels looked at her with disdain, clearly reeling from her refusal of him and her sure lesbian love with Megan. He grunted and defensively crossed his arms across his chest before leaning back heavily in his chair.

"That said, it's clear we didn't cover enough ground today. And, as many of you know, we encountered a number of the crazed individuals who ultimately had to be taken down. Lieutenant, I understand you had an issue as well?"

"There was no problem," Daniels scoffed.

"That was Carl. That creep," Norah scowled, sniffing her nose sharply. "He had it coming."

Clay withheld a smile at the woman's words. Otherwise, the mood in the bar was grim and barren, and a single look at the doctor forced him back to his somber mood.

"Now, as you can see, our doctor here isn't feeling so hot," Clay began.

"So much for being a doctor, eh?" Ralph cried from the corner.

"That's right, baby," Connie whispered after him, his personal cheerleader.

Clay paused, gritting his teeth. "We need to make sure that we have searchers tomorrow, even without the doctor's help."

"I'll do it, son," Ralph said gleefully. "I've always wanted to kill me somebody."

"He'd be great," Megan said, rolling her eyes. Alayna and Megan shared a glance, communicating volumes between them, without saying actual words.

"Well, that settles it, then. Ralph, you'll come as Doctor Miller's replacement. And Megan, Norah, and Connie, you'll stay behind with the doctor to ensure he rests up. No working too hard, Doctor. Bed rest," Clay said, eyeing Willis once more. The doctor forced a smile, but it was clear that he was in far more pain than he'd let on earlier.

Sensing he was losing the room, Clay reached toward the liquor cabinet and grasped a bottle of Harvey's bourbon reserve. He cleared his throat, thrusting the bottle onto the bar. "In any case, the best thing we can do for ourselves right now is relax. Seeing as Harvey's not here to object, and I'm sure he won't mind anyway, I think we could all use a belt from his special selection."

"Are you mad?" Norah howled. "That bottle must be worth five hundred dollars!"

"So be it," Clay said, rather pleased with himself. He popped the top from the bottle and poured himself an initial glass, sniffing at the powerful liquid. "To Harvey. And to all of us. We'll get out of this alive. Or this stuff will kill us. One or the other."

Clay grinned, tossing the drink back and sending the bottle toward Alayna, who began to pour drinks for the rest of the group. Each accepted their crystal glasses with a sheepish smile, understanding that this foray into leisure was a false safety.

37.

After several slugs of bourbon, after champagne bottles were popped and wine bottles were uncorked, the remaining derelicts of Carterville became wildly intoxicated, high on their survival and the fact that they were left behind. "It's biblical!" Ralph continued to cry in the corner, yanking at his wife's hand. "We're left behind. Just like the Good Book said!"

"That's not how it works," Alayna spouted back, pouring wine into her half-empty glass. "You chose to stay behind. God didn't leave you here."

"That's just it," Ralph spat. "We chose, but God put it in our heads to choose that. Don't you see? You're a puppet. You don't even know that what these heathens tell you isn't true at all." He eyed Megan, who stood close to Alayna, tracing her finger against the bar and dangerously close to Alayna's breast.

Clay stood near the liquor cabinet sipping his drink, his feet shoulder-width apart, feeling the alcohol course through his system. Daniels appeared beside him, his eyes exhibiting a glossy sheen.

"Sheriff," he said curtly.

"Lieutenant," Clay answered, swiping the back of his hand across his lips. "What can I do you for?"

"Ha. Now you sound like him," Daniels said,

eyeing Ralph.

"He's quite a character, isn't he?" Clay asked. "We've got a motley collection of individuals here. I saw Norah take a shot of bourbon faster than anyone else, and she took it like a champ."

"Characters, all right," Daniels said. "You know, that Alayna's one of the most beautiful women I've ever seen. At first, I really thought she dug me. So I went for it, you know?" He sighed, almost looking human for a moment, gesturing toward Alayna and Megan, whose noses were mere inches apart. "I laid it on thick. But it just goes to show you: all the best ones are either gay or already taken. I don't have a chance in her world."

"You don't seem like a terribly romantic guy, though," Clay answered bluntly. "Didn't think it'd bother you at all. After this, you'll just be on to the next town, the next love. Alayna wouldn't have been a forever thing anyway."

"Sure. But you can't curse a man for trying," Daniels said.

A silence stretched between them. Clay took another sip of his drink as he thought about the man beside him. Sure, he was a dumbass. But Daniels was pushing himself to save Carterville, a town he had no ties to. He was handling those crazed individuals who came after his townspeople without prejudice. And he was taking an interest in some of Clay's favorites, including Alayna. Perhaps he wasn't so bad. Just misguided. Clay supposed that here, in a moment of terrible significance in his small community, he had to give people the benefit of the doubt. He reached toward the lieutenant's shoulder and clapped it heartily, like an old friend.

Connie laughed loudly, and music was bursting

from the speaker system, fueling the frivolity. The drunken lieutenant grinned, flashing his eyes toward Clay. "So. I suppose I should divulge a bit more information about our exit strategy," he said, his voice rather high, lifting over the many others in the room.

Clay frowned, resting his drink back on the bar. "What do you mean? We're going to drive out of here in a few days. I didn't think there had to be any greater plan than that."

Daniels reached into his pocket and revealed a small communication-like device, more high-tech than their walkie-talkies. He jiggled it in his hand, like he was trying to prove something. "This little puppy here will get us out of the containment zone and through the energy field that's around the town."

He was still speaking loudly, almost slurring his words. Alayna looked away from Megan and marched across the room toward them, her hands upon her belt. "I'm sorry, but what do you mean, through the energy field?"

The sudden commotion caught everyone's attention. Ralph stopped his diatribe, and Norah peered at them with narrowed eyes. Willis, from his place in an easy chair, leaned forward, interest momentarily taking over his bouts of pain.

Daniels sensed he'd messed up. He stuck the device back in his pocket, eyeing the door. The song changed to one with a heightened beat. Clay felt his heart would bump from his chest.

"I mean, it's really no big deal," Daniels said.

"If it's no big deal, then tell us about it," Alayna said, her eyes wide with anticipation.

"Yeah, sure. Okay. Before the colonel left yesterday, the energy field circling the town was modified to not only block the contagion from passing through but also to prevent humans from traversing it. Not without my device, that is."

Norah stabbed her finger through the air, livid. "What do you mean? We're locked in here . . . like dogs?"

"Hey, lady. You weren't going to leave unless we dragged you out," Daniels spouted.

Megan walked slowly to Alayna and wrapped a drunken arm around her, quivering. "This is really happening, isn't it?" she whispered. People began to speak over each other in a heat of panic.

But Clay interrupted them with a loud, angry smash of his palm upon the bar. Everyone turned rapidly toward him: their savior, the man who would put the lieutenant in his place. Clay searched for the proper words for a long time, feeling livid.

"We have to get out of here," he said.

"And we will," Daniels sighed, tapping at the device once more. "This here is our golden ticket."

"But I should have been told," Clay yelled. "I'm the sheriff of this town. These people are my responsibility." He lifted his finger and jabbed Daniels's chest. "You've done more than a disservice. You've endangered us, Adam. You're working against us."

Daniels shook his head slightly. Alayna's weight shifted, sensing Clay was blowing this out of proportion, that a combination of fear and alcohol was causing him to become volatile. No one spoke as Clay exhaled sharply, incredulous.

"Everyone," Alayna began again, her voice booming. "Go to your rooms. Get some sleep. We have a lot of ground to cover tomorrow. We don't want any stragglers. No one will be left behind."

Clay nodded and winked at Alayna before he took a final shot of bourbon. Then, he meandered toward the door, his hand grasping the frame, before he shot down the hallway and toward his bedroom, with its single, lonely bed. He collapsed onto the mattress, feeling as if he were diving into a pool, and closed his eyes easily.

Panic and shock would follow him deep into his dreams. The feeling of being a wild animal locked in a cage, bucking at the constraints, gave him cold sweats, and he woke up to tug his shirt from his aching back. On his arms, the lesions oozed blood and pus. With the moonlight streaming in from the window across his blanketed legs, he felt like the loneliest person on the planet.

38.

Clay stumbled into the hallway at around five in the morning, bringing his palm across his thin head of hair. His stomach felt stretched and fizzing after too much alcohol, reminiscent of his college days, when his only cure had been fast food. He found himself in the kitchen, monitoring the gurgling coffee machine and sipping the dark liquid, waiting for something to change.

Alayna appeared in the doorway of the kitchen some ten minutes later, almost as if she'd sensed him. She yawned, showing her bright, white teeth. "Hey, Sheriff," she said. She kept her distance, as though she still sensed his anger from the previous evening.

"Don't worry, Alayna," he said, leaning heavily against the counter. "I've calmed down since last night. And I'm sorry for overreacting like that. Tensions are so high right now, you know. I feel a little frantic."

"Yeah, sure," Alayna whispered. "We all have regrets." Her voice was far away, lost.

"Did something happen?"

"Another fight," Alayna said, shivering. She eyed her socked feet. "I was so happy to see her. But then I got angry, demanding, in drunken words, why she'd stayed behind when my orders had been to get out of town. She was pissed that I thought I could 'order her around.'" She rolled her eyes slightly. "But I told her she obviously didn't know what she was talking about."

"Which, I'm guessing, didn't go over too well," Clay said, giving her a sad grin.

"You've been married a long time, I guess," Alayna agreed. She paused, sipping her coffee. "How are you feeling, by the way? Doesn't look like you've got the sweats any longer."

Clay had hardly noticed. "It does seem like I'm in some kind of remission," he said, shrugging. "The only pain I have is now just related to all that bourbon. Damn it, Harvey," he joked, hoping to mask his own fear of truly being infected.

"It's horrible. They never mentioned how much you want to get drunk when you think all is lost," Alayna said. "But it's really the first thing you want to do. To forget."

Clay nodded slightly but kept his thoughts to himself.

Moments later, Ralph and Connie appeared, looking chipper, as if they drank like that all the time. They began bickering, with Ralph cutting in front of Connie and pouring his cup of coffee first. Connie balked back, insisting that he didn't care about her feelings—that if those "monsters" out there ever attacked them, he would push her ahead and leave her for dead. Ralph didn't disagree. Alayna and Clay ignored them, turning back to the heat of their own brimming coffee cups. As they sipped, the rest of the crew joined them, searching through the meat and cheese drawers, cracking eggs, and formulating a breakfast—enough for everyone to feel nourished for the long day ahead.

It became obvious that the one person who hadn't joined them thus far was Megan. Alayna leaned heavily against the wall, unable to eat, even as the smell of the eggs and cheese and meat steamed through the air. Clay, who had joined her, heard her stomach rumble, and he held a piece of ham out toward her.

"Where is she?" he asked. "You spent the night together, right? Even though you were fighting?"

Alayna shook her head. She tapped the coffee mug back on the countertop, noting that everyone had turned toward her, waiting for her answer.

"Don't look at me," Alayna snapped, ensuring everyone could hear her. "She slept somewhere else last night." She shifted her weight, allowing the silence to boom in the kitchen.

But Daniels soon swamped over it, his voice heavy. "Well, I guess it's time for me to fess up." He rested his hands on either side of his waist, assessing Alayna, his eyes glassy and alien. "But she came to me of her own goddamn will."

"You think I don't know where she went?" Alayna said, scoffing. "I saw her drift toward your drunken form early this morning, sometime after two. You looked like a complete mess, like a broken man cradling your whiskey bottle."

"Now isn't the time for insults," Daniels said, hunching his shoulders.

"Well then, where the hell is she, if you were the last person to see her?" Clay demanded. He had to regain control.

"When I woke up this morning, she was gone," Daniels shrugged, eyeing the doorframe, visibly wishing for Megan to arrive. "Just like that."

"I suppose you two slept together, then," Alayna

said, her eyes wet.

The silence stretched on once more. In the corner, the green Doctor Miller began to cough. Spittle propelled from his mouth and dribbled down his shirt. Connie happened to notice and tended to him promptly. Clay looked on and felt utterly useless. He knew the sooner they combed through the town, the sooner they all could get the hell out. Irritated, he wondered if Megan was somewhere upstairs, holding up the process.

"No. I mean, I don't think so," Daniels said then. "We just talked. We finished off some fucking whiskey. And then—I must have passed out." He coughed, rubbing at his near-bald scalp. "It wasn't anything like that."

"Sure," Alayna said, her eyebrows high. "As if you've given me any reason to believe you."

"Believe me," Daniels said. "I was lying on the same spot on the floor in my bedroom when I woke up. The same spot on the floor I was when I last remember talking with her."

Alayna fumed with anger. She spun toward the door, visibly shaken. "I'm going to go look in your room myself, if you're so sure about this. I have to make sure you didn't do anything to her. You're a stranger to us, here, Adam. You could be a monster, for all we know."

She flashed her eyes toward him a final time before pounding up the steps, her back stiff, as the rest of the team gazed after her.

"Is this just how all lesbians act?" Ralph asked, coughing.

"Don't be so crude," Norah said, prodding him with a single, bony finger. She filled her coffee cup and balked at Daniels, showing yellowed, coffee-stained teeth. "Aren't you going to go after her? Show her everything's all right? You're a lieutenant, here, Adam. And it seems you're the one who's causing all the problems."

Daniels eyed the old woman briefly before drifting toward the doorway and out into the hotel. He bounded up the steps to follow Alayna, leaving Clay and the rest of the team below.

Clay shoved his fists into his pockets, feeling each of Daniels's steps on the rickety staircase, hoping they'd find Megan without delay—and that they could work quickly so they could join their loved ones far, far away.

"Lesbian bullshit," Ralph spat in the corner before chewing a slab of salty ham. "There's a reason we don't mess with them at the church. God didn't want them to stay alive."

"Quiet," Clay growled, his voice harsh. "I'll take none of that bullshit here."

The team stood frozen, their ears straining to catch any sounds from upstairs. A single, harsh scream sounded out, causing Clay's heart to burst against his ribcage. It was clear that the camaraderie of the previous evening had diminished, leaving only bumping headaches and wretched hangovers. He yearned for the end of the nightmare.

39.

Daniels appeared in the kitchen doorway moments later, his eyes wide. "Sheriff, we have a situation."

Clay brought his hand to his gun, sensing more of the crazed crawling through the streets, their teeth aching for blood. "What is it?"

Alayna appeared beside Daniels then. She shuddered with panic. Together they looked like twins, joined with a common, terrible truth. "She's gone," she blurted, biting her lip.

Daniels swallowed harshly, then, in a booming voice that echoed across the kitchen, said, "Megan is nowhere to be found. But that's not the worst of it."

Alayna nearly collapsed beside him, her knees bucking forward. Norah gasped, rushing forward and wrapping her frail arms around her. "Darling, get ahold of yourself," she whispered. "Jesus."

"I—I can't believe she'd do this to me . . . again," Alayna braced herself. "I thought she was past her issues . . ." she said, her voice trailing off.

Beside her, Daniels wrapped his arms around both Norah and Alayna, ensuring they remained standing. "We checked all the rooms. Megan's gone—along with the device."

"What?" Clay asked, stepping forward. "The device that was meant to—"

"To free us from this containment zone. Yes," Daniels said, finishing Clay's observation.

"You must have misplaced it," Ralph said, eyeing him haughtily. "Maybe you left it up in the bar last night?"

Daniels didn't turn toward him. "The device is gone, Sheriff."

Clay felt the internal terror rally once more. "Where the hell could it have gone, then, Daniels?"

"I suggest that Megan might have taken it, sir," Daniels answered, standing at full attention now.

"NO!" Alayna screeched beside him. "She may be deceitful at times, but she'd no more leave us in a perilous situation than I would."

Clay's team had begun to panic, quaking with fear about their sudden entrapment. "How are we going to get out?" Connie rasped. Willis inhaled sharply and leaned heavily against the refrigerator door. Norah turned her sharp eyes toward the sheriff, searching for answers.

"CALM DOWN!" Clay yelled. He brought hands to his temple, feeling sweat beads begin to form, just as they had when he'd been ill the previous day. "Megan probably just went back to her house, where she feels safe." He swallowed, his mind spinning. He didn't want to blame Alayna for this unforeseen development, and he didn't have the right to blame Daniels. "We can't get bogged down with all this drama and nonsense. It'll literally kill us. And I can promise you that."

No one spoke. Alayna seemed to regain a sense of urgency and self. She blinked madly at Clay, waiting for the remainder of his instructions.

Clay used the silence to check his wristwatch, noting the time. "Megan can't have walked far, anyway. And we still have plenty of time to clear this town before the fumigation begins. I say we continue working as we have been, and we allow Megan to get her head back on her shoulders and rejoin us here. If any of us comes across her on our search, then try and reel her in. What do you say?"

Ralph smacked his palms together, seemingly activated by Clay's words. The others calmed, nodding primly. Only Alayna seemed unchanged. She took a step from the doorway, eyeing Clay with manic eyes.

"I don't think you know what you're asking me to do here, Clay. I can't let her remain out there like this, on her own."

"Alayna," Clay said, incredulous. "You're my deputy. I need you out there, more than ever."

Alayna rested her hand on her gun. "And you know I have your back—outside of this. But I have to go after her. I can't have her out there dying, just because of me." Before Clay could respond, Alayna fled from the kitchen.

"Shit," Clay whispered, chewing at a bit of dried skin on his right thumb, watching Alayna's black hair flit from her tight bun and fly through the air as she ran.

"Let her go!" Ralph cried, filling another cup of coffee. "She's a tough one. I can tell. She can handle herself."

But Clay's stomach clenched with instant fear as he remembered the rapid pace of the crazed monsters who were clearly intent on murder.

He couldn't afford to lose his deputy.

40.

Awkward silence fell in the kitchen in the moments after Alayna's outburst. The remaining clan eyed each other with apprehension. Lieutenant Daniels began to pace back and forth, his shoulders hunched and his eyes on the floor, muttering to himself. As his murmurs grew more insistent, he began to scare the other survivors.

"If we don't have the device," Willis said, his voice quivering, "that means we don't have a way to get out?"

"We won't survive," Connie rasped, as if she was taking a stand for the truth—confident that no one else would. "We don't have a godforsaken chance."

Daniels pounded his fist against the kitchen's cinder block wall. The noise boomed through Clay's ears. Blood spit out from Daniels's knuckles, spattering across the white paint.

"Lieutenant. Get ahold of yourself!" Clay said, rushing toward him and gripping his shoulders firmly. "It's you and me here, man," he whispered into his ear. "I can't have you going AWOL on me. These people are looking to us. We're meant to lead."

Daniels's breath came jaggedly. His muscles were tense, his eyes darting toward the door every few seconds. "We have to go after her," he whispered. "She isn't safe."

Clay flung Daniels's massive body against the wall, forcing him to look in his eyes. "Lieutenant, I need you to listen. We'll find them. Both Alayna and Megan. But we need to continue searching for other stragglers as well. If Alayna's looking for Megan, and if we're all looking for Alayna, then we won't have time to find everyone. Not before. Besides, Alayna's a strong woman. If anyone can find Megan, it's her. She'll bring her back, and hopefully with the device." He swallowed hard. "I was put in charge of this town years ago, and that means I have a commitment to ensure that the people of Carterville find safety, even if they're too obtuse to follow orders."

His words hung in the air for a moment before Ralph spat on the ground, anger rattling through him. "What the hell are you talking about, Sheriff? You think me and Connie are too stupid to follow orders? Is that how you really feel?"

Clay released his hold on Daniels and turned slowly toward the people in the kitchen. Norah and Willis had joined forces near the large walk-in freezer, while Ralph and Connie looked frazzled, holding each other's aging hands and glaring at him.

"Of course not," Clay said, realizing he'd marched directly into hot water.

"Cause we had no reason to trust the government," Connie said angrily. "Why in the world would we follow orders if the rest of our lives have gone to shit, all because of the police? They took our son away three times when he was just a confused juvenile. Three times!" Her eyes lacked emotion, but her voice was haughty, strong. "Why in the world would we trust you?"

"Because I'm all you have," Clay offered, his voice bursting over hers. "And I'm going to make sure you get out. But I need your help finding the rest of them. The rest of the people who, like you, didn't take this issue as seriously as they should have. We don't have to make this a tragedy. But we have to work together."

"Still don't have the device," the doctor whispered from the corner.

Clay made his hands into fists, suddenly feeling that the world was working against him. As he steamed with anger, Willis began to slide down the walk-in freezer door, his eyes closing quickly. Norah knelt down to grasp his shoulder and shake him.

"He's green, Sheriff," she whispered. "He's not looking good."

Clay rushed toward the man and felt for his pulse, noting that, despite his pale complexion and lack of energy, his heart was beating erratically. His own heart flipped with panic. "Get him some water," he ordered, jiggling the man's shoulder, trying to make him regain consciousness. "Come on!"

Connie moved forward with a glass of water, and together they helped the doctor sip it through his dry, cracked lips. His exhaustion prevented him from opening his eyes.

Clay held his position, gazing up at the other survivors as the doctor continued to drink. "All right," he said. "I understand your frustration. I really do. You all know that it's my duty to find as many townspeople as possible. And Lieutenant Daniels, I need you with me. We'll start by going back to Megan's house first, and then stopping by Alayna's. But know this: we're going to keep looking for the left behind."

"Sure thing," Daniels affirmed, giving the sheriff a stern salute.

"In the meantime, I need all of you to watch out for Doctor Miller, here." Clay paused, contemplating how to handle his suspicions about the doctor without overtly alarming everyone. "Most of us have seen what this crazed infection does to a person," Clay said as his gaze drifted over the doctor. "We all need to remain sharp and prepared for action. Can you do that? Can you protect yourselves, as well as the rest of us?"

Connie looked at Ralph for direction, but before she could respond, Norah spoke.

"You can count on me, Sheriff. I may be old, but I know how to handle my share of cooking utensils," she said, gripping the cast iron pan she'd just used to make everyone breakfast and hoisting it high above her head. "If he turns, I'll make sure it goes no further."

The kitchen remained silent for several moments as Norah's words sank in.

"One more thing," Clay said. "Keep your eyes on the door. Alayna and Megan could come back to the hotel at any time. Watch out for them. And stick together."

He jumped to his feet and headed toward the door, adjusting his holster. He felt Daniels's presence behind him, and they marched toward the hotel entrance, retreating from the glowing kitchen and the homey scent of breakfast.

Main Street appeared before him, abandoned, a forgotten wasteland. Not a single animal, bug, or human remained in sight. Alayna and her vehicle were gone.

"You ready for this, Sheriff?" Daniels asked him as the hotel door clicked closed, leaving them out in the desolate environment. "Because I think if that was any indication, today is going to be a shit show."

"We don't have a choice," Clay answered, marching from the front porch and past the rocking chairs. He opened the car gruffly, feeling a bit of his right arm lesion begin to break open—a constant reminder that his body was failing him minute by minute, along with his crew. He paused, his mind spinning.

"Sheriff?" Daniels asked, hesitating before opening the passenger side. "Everything all right?"

"I didn't think this was what it would look like," Clay murmured, knowing he sounded just as insane as the others. "I didn't imagine this at all."

"None of us did," Daniels said, shrugging his muscled shoulders. "As my grandmother said, moments before she drew her final breath: this wasn't in the cards."

41.

"It wasn't what you think," Daniels began the moment Clay punched the gas pedal and raced through town. "With Megan and me. It wasn't what you think."

"I don't know what the hell to think anymore," Clay said, cutting through a turn. He didn't bother to stop at signs, to follow any speed limit. He felt overwhelmed, unable to fully comprehend Daniels's words.

But he continued. "After you left the bar last night, I wasn't going to hang around long, but I had more drinking to do. When I was with my last unit, that's all I liked to do, really. Take comfort in a little liquid solace."

"I see," Clay said, eyeing the horizon. He thought he glimpsed a figure staggering through the cornfield. One of the crazed or a scarecrow? But he continued to barrel toward their first stop, hopeful he wouldn't be required to blast a bullet through another homicidal brain.

"Then Megan came to my room. Alayna was chasing after her, telling her to come back to bed. Telling her that they should talk things out. I don't know what the fuss was all about," Daniels said, scoffing. "But Megan took one look at me and, with a devilish smile, she came in the room, sat down beside me, poured herself a drink, and just glared up at Alayna."

"Megan's been known to be a little too spirited at times," Clay said. "Alayna seems to understand her well enough to know what's right or wrong. She's told me on more than one occasion that they're soul mates, they belong together."

"I'm not so sure, Clay," Daniels continued, scratching at the stubble spreading across his chin. "Because the minute Megan sat down, she began to flirt. I mean, really laying it on heavy. She wanted me, you see."

Clay forced himself not to roll his eyes. "Don't you say that about every woman?" he asked, feeling the awkwardness of his words.

Daniels glared. "Megan wanted me. She touched my chest. She leaned toward me with her big, supple lips. Man, she was good. She was hot. She was everything I dreamed of in a woman, there in front of me."

"I thought you said Alayna was everything you dreamed of in a woman?" Clay mocked.

"Whatever. That was then. This was now," Daniels said, looking out the side window. "Where we going, anyway? Haven't we been out here already?"

Clay had the gas pedal floored, and the speedometer clicked just past seventy as he blazed past the high school. "Alayna's house isn't too far from here. Maybe she went there first, hoping to find Megan waiting for her."

"Where's the logic with that? If we're looking for the girls first, Megan's place is where we should start. She left last night, on foot. My money is on her heading home to get her wheels, get gas, and then get out of town."

Clay usually had better judgement in situations like this, and he was irritated with himself that the big military oaf had outsmarted him.

"Damn it!" Clay spat, then slammed on the brakes and swerved the car to the side of the road before cranking the wheel hard to the left. Moments later, they were speeding back in the direction they had just come, heading for Megan's.

"Anyway," Daniels continued, "Megan really opened my eyes last night. She really might be the one."

Clay sighed heavily. "Whatever. It's none of my business at all what you do, or what Megan does, or what Alayna thinks. None of it's my business."

"Well, Alayna stormed off after that," Daniels said. "And like I said, I don't think anything happened."

Clay couldn't speak. He was uncomfortable, his stomach straining with worry for Alayna, and for Megan. As he came upon the next intersection, something caught his eye. It happened in a flash, but he was positive what he saw. "Sonofabitch!" he snapped as he slammed on the brakes.

"What is it, Sheriff?" Daniels asked, gripping his gun with one hand and holding the door handle with the other. He was ready.

"Easy, there. I just saw two more stragglers through that picture window right there." Clay pointed to the house on the corner. Inside, shadows could be seen dancing along the stark wall, cast there by the glow of the television.

"You sure? Could be someone just left the boob tube on," Daniels remarked.

"Only one way to find out," Clay said as he flung his car door wide. "Let's make this quick, though. The longer we waste here, the farther away Megan might get."

42.

Alayna sprang from her patrol car and ran up to Megan's front porch. She clenched her fist and pounded wildly upon the wooden door. "Open up, Megan. It's me, Al," she said as she brought her face close to the side window. She saw no movement in the desolate interior.

"Damn it," she cursed as she leaped from the porch and bound around to the back of the house. There, next to the rear stoop, sat a gallon-sized clay pot with amber colored gardenias growing in it. Alayna kicked the pot over with her booted foot, expecting to find the seldom-used brass key lying on the ground. It was gone. Alayna's heart sank. "No!"

Alayna gripped the handle of the wooden screen door and yanked it wide. She again pounded on the door, loud enough to wake the dead. "God damn it, Megan! Open the fucking door!"

Silence.

"Don't make me kick the door in!" Alayna demanded. There was again no reply. She took two steps back and charged the back door, slamming her foot right next to the door latch. In another time, Alayna would've been gleeful at her sudden badass abilities, but now was not the time.

The door imploded, leaving splinters of wood scattered along the floor just inside. Alayna crossed the threshold into Megan's kitchen. She walked through the dining room before turning left into the living room, her eyes shifting wildly about the place, looking for a something, anything, that indicated that Megan was there. It was like no one had ever existed there at all.

Moving into the hallway, she opened all the bedroom doors and the bathroom. It was as if any personal belongings were cleared out long ago. "No!" Alayna yelled. "Where have you gone?"

Angry, Alayna retraced her steps back to the living room and noticed a handwritten note lying on the coffee table. *Could she have?* Alayna wondered as she slowly picked it up and began to read.

Al-

I'm sorry. I know this is not your fault. Trust me when I tell you that it's me. It's not you at all. I'm afraid of what we could have been together and considering the recent happenings in this town, I'm not sure I'm strong enough. I'm going away and I don't want you to follow. I think it's better this way. Again, I'm sorry.

Megan

She wiped fleeting tears from her eyes and dropped the paper back to the coffee table. "Why?" she whispered.

Alayna slowly made her way back to her car. Slouching behind the steering wheel, she tried to think of where Megan might've gone. There was something about the note that didn't sit well with her. Why write a note at all? Why not just leave if that's really what she wanted? *She wants me to chase after her. That must be it!* But where would she have gone?

Alayna turned over the ignition and revved her way out onto the street. As she began her aimless drive, her mind scrubbed through her and Megan's past. Maybe she'd go someplace that had meaning for them both. Maybe she'd go and wait for her. But where?

As Alayna came to the next intersection, she looked left and then right, waiting for the nonexistent traffic to give her the go. She finally accelerated, and suddenly it hit her. "The park!" It was a quick drive from where she was, and it was where they'd first met. That had to be it.

Alayna cranked hard on the wheel and sped toward her new destination. With each passing moment, Alayna knew she was right. She had to be. She wouldn't allow Megan just to walk away from her like that.

A normal five-minute drive turned into less than two minutes. Alayna screeched to a halt at the edge of the park, threw open her door, and began running through the park. She felt so positive that that's where Megan would be. She had to be. She continued down the trail and through a cluster of aspen trees. She ran past the rock outcropping that had been vandalized many years before with juvenile graffiti. As she crested the hill, the park bench came into view. Alayna's heart dropped as she saw that it was empty.

The adrenaline flowing through her body continued to drive her forward, all the way up to the bench itself. She stood in front of it, looking down at the painfully vacant seat. Her hands trembled as she lowered herself to the creaky wooden surface. "Damn it, Megan," she whispered. "Why? Why leave, why now?"

There was no answer.

Alayna sat on their park bench and stared out

across the hilly valley. She remembered back to the moment they'd first met. It wasn't really all that long ago, and at the time, Alayna had been confused about her own sexuality. She'd just been through a breakup with her on-again, off-again boyfriend when she found Megan there, walking her dog. She'd been so friendly and so vibrant that Alayna was instantly attracted to her.

More tears flowed from Alayna's eyes as her mind drifted from her solitary present and into a fruitful past. She remembered the first trip they'd taken, to a cabin up by Lake Cornwell. It was the first time they'd been intimate with each other, and it was a moment she'd never forget.

43.

Clay and Daniels burst into the house without the pretense of knocking. Time was of the essence, and the hour for strict procedures had passed.

Clay bound forward to discover two teenagers, a boy and a girl, eating beef jerky and watching a movie on an antiquated VCR, their eyes grey and grim. They glared at the intruders but then swept their eyes back to the screen. “Don’t interrupt,” the boy whispered. “It’s the best part.”

Incredulous, Clay spat, “Hey. Kids. You’re going to have to come with us.”

The boy, who had an Asian-language tattoo traced on his skinny upper bicep, smiled with dingy teeth. “And I suppose you have some kinda plan to make us leave?”

“Don’t you know what’s going on? The town needs to be evac—”

“Yeah, we know,” the boy interrupted. “Our parents were killed on our way out of town. And if we’re going to die too, then we’d just as soon be in our house when our fate arrives.”

Clay swallowed. “Your parents were killed?”

“Those people,” the girl said, her voice barely quivering. “I can’t describe them. We were at the stoplight. Me and Brandon here were in the back seat, eating licorice and talking about our future in

Florida. You know, I've always wanted to go to Florida, and here was my opportunity. But some asshole just came up and bit my dad's ear off. And then he ate the rest of his face from his skull, leaving just dripping bones." She said it matter-of-factly, cracking her gum as she spoke.

"And then, of course, Mom went wild," the boy said. "Brittany and I got out and just ran back here. We didn't know where else to go."

"Well, we made a stop at the grocery and grabbed some things on the way," Brittany said, tossing a Cheetos toward the sheriff. "And if we die here, we'll die with dignity. Not running away."

Clay eyed the Cheetos rolling toward him on the dirty carpet. If he didn't know better, he'd assumed the kids in front of him were high on some recreational drug that had been running around the teen community. "I'm sorry about your parents," he said, his voice rasping. "But you don't have to die, you know? It's my job to get you out of here. To get you to safety."

"HA!" Brandon said. "Safety doesn't exist any longer." His words drifted into a fit of laughter.

Daniels stepped forward and grabbed the boy by his upper arms, lifting him heartily into the air. The boy began to shake, his feet inches from the ground. "Hey! Let go of me!" his laughter turned to cries, panic tingeing his cheeks red. "Get the fuck out of our house!"

But Daniels didn't let go. He flung the boy over his shoulder, lifted the bag of chips from the coffee table, and then marched outside.

44.

Alayna rode in the passenger seat of Megan's SUV, fidgeting nervously. "I don't understand, Meg. Why all the hush-hush?"

"Because, silly. It was three weeks ago today that we happened to meet. And I have something special planned."

Alayna sighed. Being a deputy for so many years, she was not accustomed to being kept in the dark. It did not sit well with her, and perhaps maybe that was why she had never found a lifelong mate. She had trust issues, and now, suddenly being on the verge of dipping her toe in the waters with another woman, she was apprehensive. She didn't want to mess this up. She wanted to take this "ride" for many years, and Megan seemed like the right person to go with. She sat back and accepted her fate.

Twenty minutes later, Megan pulled up next to a rustic mountain cabin that overlooked a modest, glistening pond. "What's this?" Alayna asked.

"This," Megan said proudly, "is my old family cabin. My granddad built it many years ago, and it's been handed down through the family over the years. After my dad passed away last year, it came to me."

Alayna considered the rundown appearance of the cabin as they sat in the car. Although she wasn't a girlie girl per se, she still appreciated the comforts of a civil lifestyle. And from what she was seeing from the passenger seat of Megan's car, this was far from it. She smiled politely.

"Oh, don't worry. The outside looks like this for a reason. It keeps the vagrants away. The inside has been fully updated and remodeled. There's even a Jacuzzi tub in the master bath," Megan said as she stepped out of the car and grabbed her bag from the back seat. Alayna did the same and followed Megan up the steps to a large wraparound deck. The scenery was beautiful, she had to admit. As Megan jostled her keys around and unlocked the door, Alayna could see the edge of the lake around the side of the house. As each moment passed, so did Alayna's apprehension.

After a brief tour of the cabin's interior, Megan led Alayna out to the back deck that was perched high above the lake below. "Breathtaking, isn't it?" she asked.

Alayna sidled up next to Megan at the edge of the guardrail and peered out across the surface of the glasslike water. "It's . . . beautiful," Alayna said, completely awestruck by the view.

"I'm glad you approve," Megan said as she leaned in and kissed Alayna on the lips.

As Alayna sat on the bench overlooking the park, she remembered the feeling of Megan's lips pressed against hers as if it were just that morning. Suddenly, she sat up on the park bench and wiped her eyes dry. That's it! I know where she went! Stay where you are, baby. I'm on my way!

Alayna, full of vigor once again, ran as fast as her feet could carry her back to her cruiser and back on her chase. Her chase for Megan.

45.

Brittany sprang from her seat, shrieking, and lunged after her grappling brother. Clay tried to grab her as she passed, but she was too quick. She reached Daniels before Clay could stop her and began to pummel his sides, trying to force him to release her brother. But Daniels marched through the front door and back to the cruiser, pushing them both into the back seat and slamming the door. He turned toward Clay, who was trailing out the front door. "Let's get on with it," he boomed. "We're losing time."

Clay felt numb as he drove away from the house, the two teenagers howling with anger.

"YOU SHOULD HAVE LET US STAY. WHAT ABOUT OUR CONSTITUTIONAL RIGHTS?" Brittany screeched, grasping at the inoperable door handle and gazing out the window, tears swimming down her cheeks. "THIS IS FUCKING MESSED UP, YOU KNOW THAT? A FUCKING TRIP!"

Clay pursed his lips together, feeling more anxious with each of her pleas. Daniels pressed his fingers into his ears, throwing an apologetic glance at Clay. Clay nodded and gunned it, guiding the cruiser ahead, toward their original destination.

After several minutes of no reaction from Clay or Daniels, Brittany finally dialed her tantrum back to mere whimpers. Brandon, clearly the older of the two, sat with his arms crossed and a dazed glimmer in his eyes. More evidence of his drug euphoria, Clay considered as he took several glances in his rearview.

The minutes silently crept by, and Daniels continued to scan the landscape whisking by the side window, looking for more survivors. None were in sight.

Finally, Clay screeched the cruiser to a halt in front of Megan's place.

"Um, just where are you taking us, anyway?" Brandon asked, gazing out at the abandoned streets.

Clay gripped his door handle, then paused. He contemplated how much he should tell them. "Eventually we're going to get you to the hotel at the center of town. That's where everyone else is. But first we need to track down a few people that—"

"Cool! Is this a bust? Can we come?" Brittany begged, suddenly showing interest as opposed to mere agitation.

"Not this time, kids," Daniels said firmly. "We'll only be a minute. You two can wait here."

"Fucking pigs. Can you at least roll our windows down so we don't suffocate?" she said, throwing an evil glare at Daniels.

With an irritated sigh, Clay keyed the controls and lowered the back two windows several inches. "Better?" He didn't wait for a response.

Moments later, Clay and Daniels stepped up to the front door. It was open a crack. Clay rested his hand on his holster, thumbing the leather strap free before gently nudging the door fully open.

"Hello? Is anyone here? Alayna, it's Clay," he said as he strode into Megan's living room. He scanned the room as Daniels blasted by and began searching the rest of the house. Clay sensed something was not right, but he couldn't put his finger on it. He continued to scrutinize every detail of the scene when Daniels returned from the bedroom hallway.

"I got nothin', boss," he said before moving into the dining room and then into the kitchen. Clay noticed Megan's letter and began to read when suddenly Daniels called out. "Sherriff! You've got to see this!"

Clay quickly finished the short note to Alayna then hurried to see what Daniels was carrying on about.

"Something went down here," Daniels said as he pointed out the shards of splintered wood near the back door. "Looks like somebody wanted in that wasn't supposed to be here.

"Doesn't add up," Clay said. "The house is nearly cleared out of personal belongings, and then this? Do you think Alayna found Megan already and took her back to the hotel?"

"If she did, you'd think they'd have radioed us to tell us as much."

Clay nodded silently and stepped out into the backyard. As he did so, he heard an ear-splitting crash echoing between the houses. Before he could react, Daniels ran by and shimmied up next to the edge of the house, his weapon drawn and the safety off. Slowly, he inched his face around the corner and peered into the side yard.

"Are you kidding me?" he bellowed.

46.

Clay rushed ahead and saw what Daniels was so exasperated about. The back door of his cruiser was ajar, and broken glass was scattered about the ground.

"Those stupid kids," Daniels yelled.

"Easy, Adam. They're just frightened and are probably in some form of mild shock. They did just lose their parents in a really gruesome way, remember?"

Daniels sighed. "Yeah, I suppose. But this is something we don't have time for. We need to find those girls and get that device."

"We will. But first things first. Let's round the kids up and drop them at the hotel before we go back out," Clay said, his mind reeling with thoughts of Alayna. "And if we can't find that damn device, we'll just have to figure another way out."

Without time to completely analyze Clay's thoughts on escaping the containment zone, they returned to the cruiser and began searching for the teens.

"We really should split up and search through the nearest houses. That's where I'd go if I was wanting to hide," Daniels said.

"Normally I'd agree with you, but I don't think that's where they'd go. I think it's much more simple than that. They're stoned off their asses and probably not able to think straight," Clay said as he steered the cruiser onto the roadway.

"Stoned, like on drugs?" Daniels asked, apparently shocked at the concept.

"Didn't you see the signs? Eyes dilated, the mood swings? They're probably both so high to try to deal with the severity of this entire fucked-up situation."

Daniels sat in silence as Clay's words sunk in. "Hell, maybe we should find some drugs and take their approach."

Clay chuckled. The thought certainly had its merits. "If only it were that easy," he said, the memories of the previous night flooding his thoughts.

Over the next few hours, the duo searched. They slowly drove up and down every street in the vicinity. They'd occasionally see what appeared to be movement in the distance, but each time it turned out to just be the rustling of trees or shrubs caused by the unusually harsh wind.

When all appeared to be lost, Clay changed directions entirely. He pulled out of Megan's subdivision and headed to the far side of town.

"So, we giving up, then?" Daniels asked.

"Not quite. If you were alone and afraid, where would you go? Someplace familiar—someplace safe. We're going back to where we picked them up."

Several minutes later, they turned onto the street where the teens had lived, and sure enough, two people were walking along the middle of the road, just a few houses away from their destination. Clay noticed Daniels nodding his head, relieved. "Now what?" he asked.

"Now we grab them again, and this time we don't let them out of our sight."

Clay glanced at his watch and was surprised just how much time they'd already spent away from the hotel. It was nearing three in the afternoon, and he hoped the teens would not try to evade them, wasting more precious time.

Thankfully, his concerns were unwarranted. As he pulled his cruiser alongside of the walking siblings, he noticed their euphoric state had been replaced with utter fear. They stopped walking as Clay slowed his vehicle. Without any semblance of protest, Brandon and Brittany climbed into the back of the vehicle and slammed the door.

"Just so you know, we're only going with you because you'd keep coming for us otherwise," Brittany said, her face screwed up into an ugly frown. "And as soon as we're out of this town, we're on our own again, you hear?"

Clay pursed his lips together, feeling more anxious with each of her words. Daniels remained stoic, staring ahead. Clay simply nodded as he eyed the gas station on the main road, noting he needed to fill his tank before roving the rest of the way through town. He pulled over, grateful to be outside of the car, doing something as familiar as filling his gas tank.

Daniels appeared beside him, his eyes on the horizon. Always, it seemed, they were watching for danger. "That was easier than I'd expected," he whispered.

"I think they're still in shock," Clay muttered. "I didn't know so many people had been killed already. We haven't seen many dead bodies, and they're probably scared of being alone."

"Could be hidden, I guess," Daniels said, nodding. "Hard to say."

Suddenly Brandon began pounding on the window, his eyes popping wide. “HEY!” he cried. “HEY!”

Fuel continued to pump into the gas tank. Clay turned toward them, rolling his eyes. But he popped open the back, his fingers tracing his gun in his holster. “Hey there,” he said. “What seems to be the problem?”

“Brittany has to pee,” Brandon said, scoffing. “We’re allowed to do that, at least, aren’t we?”

Clay eyed the empty gas station. “Will you walk her in?” he asked Daniels, shrugging. “We can’t take the chance that they’ll escape again.”

47.

Daniels walked with Brittany toward the entrance, opened the door for her, and took a position outside. As they waited, a wind blasted from the west, whipping at Clay's face and causing him to feel strained, fatigued, like all they were doing was for naught.

"You can't keep us like this," Brandon called from the back seat again, a final plea.

"I think you'll like the others," Clay said, trying to be reasonable. "We're all in this together, now. Nobody's getting left behind."

"Ha," Brandon said, punching the back of the front seat violently. "You say it like you know how to make it all go away."

As Clay stared at Brandon, realizing the truth of his statement, he heard a gut-wrenching scream from deep inside of the gas station. He rushed toward the door, listening as the gas pump began to spurt gas onto the pavement. He hadn't bothered to click it off. Brandon chased after, his tennis shoes sloshing through the river of gasoline and his voice ringing out, "BRITTANY!"

Daniels entered the gas station first, Clay and Brandon following close behind. They gasped for air as they stood near the window, watching as several of the crazed swarmed around Brittany, tearing into her shoulders, her stomach, her thighs. She screamed with panic, grasping at their faces and hair, tossing their dead curls to the ground. She'd popped one of them in the eye with her finger, and the eye was now bobbing along on the floor, coating the tiles with slime.

"NO!" Brandon cried, thrusting himself forward.

Clay gripped him and forced him back and out of danger. Panic then drove him forward, reaching for his gun. Daniels followed. As they entered the chip and pretzel aisle, a few of the crazed separated from the gluttonous horde and began to charge toward them. Clay and Daniels lifted their guns to the crazed monsters' freakish heads, shooting them swiftly in succession, causing them to crash against the pile of melting ice in the corner. As the thunderous shots echoed throughout the confined space, Brittany couldn't maintain her defensive stance near the bathroom. She bucked back against the wall, her skull bouncing dully, before she slid down the white wall, trailing a stark, crimson line. The moment she landed, her jaw dropped open, revealing a dollop of green goop on her sickish tongue.

Clay reached her first, noting the depth of her injuries. Her brother, Brandon, was in a heap near the doorway, screeching. "THEY GOT HER, TOO! THEY GOT HER." He wept, clenching his hands together, making one giant fist. "NO!"

Daniels knelt beside Clay, checking the girl's pulse. He dropped her chilly arm quickly, making a motion toward the door. "I didn't know they were in here," he muttered. "I made a quick check before I let her in."

"Were they hiding?" Clay asked, wondering what kind of intelligence they were dealing with. "Did they see us coming up the road?" He eyed the almost-humans splayed in bloody heaps around them. "Jesus. This is too fucking much."

"I don't know," Daniels whispered. "I just don't know."

Behind them, Brandon had stopped screeching. His inhales came sharply, cutting into their ears. "We should get him back to the hotel," Clay said, jolting to his feet. "Out of here."

As they gathered Brandon and eased him back toward the car, he fought against their restraining arms, attempting to lunge toward his sister's dead body. But Clay and Daniels held him firmly.

"She wouldn't have died if you hadn't made us leave," Brandon whimpered, leaning heavily against the car. Around them, the gasoline had split into many different rivers and capillaries, churning toward the road. "She never would have died."

"Kid, that's where you're wrong," Daniels spouted. "She would have, and so would you. Now you owe it to her to keep yourself alive." He prodded the kid's chest with a dominating finger before shoving him quickly into the Naugahyde-covered seats. "Clay. We should go."

Clay nodded, rushing toward the driver's seat. As he ran, he heard the familiar beeps of his walkie-talkie, still attached to his side.

"Sheriff? Clay?" The voice was familiar, causing his heart to warm instantly. "Are you there? Over."

Clay lifted the walkie-talkie, making momentary eye contact with Daniels. "Alayna. Copy. God, it's good to hear from you. Where the hell are you?"

"I'm fine. I'm fine," she said, her voice sounding haggard. "I need to make this quick. Clay, you need to gather everyone from the hotel and bring them out to the edge of town. That's where the energy field is."

"Which edge of town?"

"Out past the Crawford farm. Where it all began," Alayna said. "Clay. Come quickly. I can't stress this enough."

In that moment, the walkie-talkie halted its crackle and an eerie silence settled in. Before long, the glare from Lieutenant Daniels and the teenage boy howling with pain and terror in the back seat finally spurred Clay ahead. Without wasting another moment, he shoved himself into the front seat and floored the accelerator, pushing them back toward the hotel, all the while praying, inwardly, that nothing else had gone wrong since they'd left.

Perhaps the nightmare was nearly over.

48.

Clay and Daniels arrived back at the hotel minutes later, leaving the car idling outside and popping open the back door, allowing Brandon to exit. He had grown catatonic in the moments after his sister's death. His jaw was clamped shut. He shivered, his eyes searching the abandoned road as he followed Clay and Daniels into the gleaming hotel foyer. Clay felt as if ages had passed since they'd left the hotel.

Norah sat in the foyer, her aging, grey eyes turned toward them. She sighed as they entered. "They're all upstairs at the bar. The doctor—he isn't going to make it. He's shivering, sweating, losing blood from his nose, mouth, and eyes."

Clay nodded, taking the information in stride. He gripped her forearm gently, feeling the dryness of her skin. "I understand, and we can sort him out in a bit. But right now, we need to go see Alayna. Can you head to one of the cars? We found another holdout, and he's already waiting out front. I'm going to gather the others."

She nodded without protest, rising to stand, her knees creaking beneath her. "The deputy. Did she find her girlfriend?"

"Don't know yet," Clay said, turning toward the steps. He felt he was living a dream, pounding from the first floor to the second, discovering Ralph and Connie pointing at each other and rehashing some argument from their past. Their eyes flashed as they screamed. They looked like raccoons.

“The doc’s not doing so hot,” Connie said, her voice blaring. It seemed she was tattling, like a girl in school.

“So I’ve heard,” Clay said. “But right now we have to get to the edge of town. Get out front. Lieutenant Daniels will drive you.”

Connie rolled her eyes but shot down the steps, racing her husband. They burst past Norah, who was still easing toward the sheriff’s car. Clay took a final look down the empty hallway, which reeked of mold and age, before skirting into the doctor’s bedroom. He quivered beneath his sheets, wrapped like a burrito and sweating profusely. His forehead and nose poked out from beneath the damp sheet, each a pale green. Clay knelt beside him, noting the terror in the doctor’s eyes. He looked like a man on the brink of insanity.

“How’s it going, Doc?” Clay breathed, reminded of the morning he’d spent with his wife the day she’d delivered Maia. “I’d say we’ve both seen better days, wouldn’t you?”

The doctor couldn’t speak. His eyes, bloodshot and irritated, fixed on Clay’s. They alone spoke volumes, and Clay knew Norah was right. He just hoped that that whatever this infection was would take the doctor peacefully, but he sensed it was a futile wish.

Clay whispered, “We’re going to leave now. But I’ll come back for you. Know that I will. All right?”

Seconds ticked along, stretching into minutes. Clay backed from the room, sensing that he’d begun looking at a corpse. He stumbled down the steps and into the empty Main Street, discovering Brandon vomiting near his cruiser and Ralph, Connie, Norah, and Daniels all piled in the military vehicle. Clay sniffed, sliding into the driver's seat and waiting for Brandon to tuck in beside him. Brandon swiped the back of his hand across his lips before tumbling in and slamming the door. Clay hurried from the hotel and down Main Street, speeding toward the edge of town. Toward the mysterious unknown.

49.

They approached the perimeter, where an energy field had formed a greenish haze encircling the town and rising up, bubble-like, toward the sky. Clay's eyes narrowed. Beside him, Brandon leaned forward, trying to spot where the bubble burst. "It's like a giant bug zapper," he whispered. "I mean—this isn't common, is it? This doesn't seem normal."

Clay didn't speak. He'd spotted Alayna's car, which she'd apparently picked up from the station, near the energy field and on the other side of the main road. She stood leaning heavily against the hood, glaring across the green film. The moment she spotted them, she popped up and waved, her face showing no sign of happiness.

Clay and Daniels parked beside her, their tires sinking into the grassy edge. The moment Clay exited his vehicle, Alayna rushed toward him and wrapped her arms around his neck, shuddering. "I'm so sorry I left like that," she whispered. "It wasn't right. I just . . . I needed to find her."

Clay patted her back soothingly. Her muscles were tense and spasming at his touch. "But did you find her?" he asked, eyeing the green horizon. "What happened?" Outside of the perimeter, several cars were rolled over, burning, spitting black fumes. He winced when he noticed people inside them.

Alayna's head drooped down. "She's nowhere to be found. I went to her house, but she had already cleared out. I tried a few other places I thought she might go, but found nothing. So I decided to come out here. I knew this had been the checkpoint. The way out of town. At least, it had been yesterday."

Clay nodded, remembering the long line of townspeople waiting to scurry from Carterville. Now the artery was desolate.

"But when I got here, I didn't find any government station, obviously," she said. "I only found that." She pointed toward the other side of the energy field, where smoke and fire burst forth from the horizon, alerting them to crisis and disaster.

"I've never seen anything like it," Clay said, taking several steps toward the energy field. He brought his palm upward, stretching his fingers along the green hue.

"Me neither. Or heard about it," Alayna whispered.

As they stood, staring wordlessly at the energy field and at the steaming, smoking vehicles strewn out on the other side, the rest of the clan all lined up beside them. Norah leaned heavily upon a makeshift cane, a stick she'd picked up somewhere along the way.

"What the hell is this?" she said with asperity.

"It's from the aliens," Connie said, her voice harsh. "What else would it be?"

No one else spoke. Alayna and Clay made eye contact, sensing that their pack of rescuees was growing panicked. Brandon began to sneer, stomping about all along the energy field edge, muttering to himself. "They just ate her," he whispered. "They just gobbled her up. Just like that. And now it's over. It's done."

"Who's the kid?" Alayna whispered to Clay.

"We picked him up at his house. His sister, she died," Clay whispered back, noting the intensity in Brandon's eyes.

"And the doctor?"

"He couldn't leave the hotel. Was still alive when we left, but . . ." Clay trailed off, eyeing Ralph and Connie off to his right, who were becoming increasingly quarrelsome. They seemed like decorations in the terror at the end of the world.

"I might as well throw you into that thing," Ralph spat at his wife, shifting his weight. "You little tramp. I know you cheated on me with Fred. After church last week, I knew where you were. You second-rate floozy."

"HA!" Connie yelled. "As if you weren't off with your little side thing two weeks ago yourself."

"How did they get on this topic?" Alayna asked Clay, allowing a simple smile to stretch across her face.

"Seems they're always fighting. It must be what they do," Clay said sadly, his eyes still far away.

But as they stood, Ralph and Connie's fight escalated. Ralph shoved at Connie, pushing her closer to the green-hued energy field. Brandon flung his fingers toward his mouth, clearly panicked. "Don't," Norah breathed, her back hunched.

"How dare you?" Connie hissed. "You want me to fly through that thing, is that it? As if it could hurt me? We're all going to die here anyway." She thrashed her finger through the air, yelling at Ralph.

"Calm down—" Alayna began, taking a step closer. "We need to stick together."

Connie turned toward Alayna, then. She seethed

with anger. “As if I should listen to you, you dyke. You abandoned all of us. You left us at that hellhole hotel. Just mind your own business.”

“Fly through that energy field for all I care!” Ralph yelled. “None of us want you here. None of us even care if you live or die.”

With that, Connie spun toward the green bubble. With her arms flailing, she rushed toward it. Daniels screamed, taking huge leaps toward her, trying to reach her. But her body hit the force field far too soon, thrashing and then suddenly disintegrating, splattering blood and viscera on either side of the green bubble. Her bones emitted a speck of light before sizzling to nothingness. One moment, Connie existed, lived, breathed, and yelled. And the next minute, her blood coated the fluttering wild flowers along the roadside.

50.

Immediately Ralph dropped to his knees. His wails echoed across the fields, booming against their vehicles. "CONNIE!" he cried, over and over again. "CONNIE. COME BACK!"

Everyone stood horrified, their hands over their mouths. Clay took several steps forward, watching as blood began to coat his boots. Alayna murmured behind him, "Clay. Don't."

He eyed the green energy field more closely, noting that it sizzled with electricity. Ralph continued to moan with anger and sadness, whimpering, Connie's name eternally on his lips. Brandon and Norah didn't move. Norah's eyes were stern, hard, as if she'd seen battle before. And Daniels moved closer to Alayna, placing a hand on her back.

"What the hell are we going to do now, Sheriff?" Brandon asked, breaking the silence. Clay turned to face the group.

As if on cue, howls and screeching rang through the air, reminiscent of the crazed monsters in the town. Clay whipped his head back toward the energy field, watching as three of the once-humans crawled from the interior of the smoking SUV at the side of the road. One had a broken neck, and his head lolled from side to side as he stretched his limbs toward them. The other two with him, both young men, began to wail and rush forward. Alayna and Daniels ran to stand beside Clay as a first line of defense. They lifted their guns.

"Shoot them in the brain," Clay said. "When they get close enough." The unarmed people in his group cowered behind the military vehicle. Ralph continued to weep.

When the approaching crazed were mere feet away, Clay swallowed sharply, his Adam's apple catching. He could see into the window of these monsters' eyes, almost sensing what kind of men they'd been before they turned into their manic forms. He was going to kill sons, fathers, brothers—men of his beautiful town. And he couldn't afford to think about it.

The moment Clay was about to shoot, the first monster blasted into the energy field. Just as Connie had done moments before, he disintegrated immediately, his crimson blood blasting like a bomb through the air. The other two followed along the same, mortal path. Their brittle bones coated the grass on either side of the energy field and splattered over Clay's pants. Clay leaped back, feeling the strength of the blast. He blinked toward Alayna, noting that her nose dripped with blood.

"What the—?" Ralph cried again. "What the hell is going on?"

But in the silence that followed, Clay couldn't find words to console his group. The crazed individuals who had been meant to remain on the inside of the energy field were now on the outside. It seemed that Colonel Wallace's plan hadn't panned out precisely as they'd all hoped.

And Clay didn't even want to consider what that meant for the rest of the world.

51.

After several minutes of stunned silence, Clay turned on his heel and strode back to his cruiser, swiping his arm through the air. “Let’s . . . get away from here. Let’s go back to the hotel,” he said. “Come on.” His hope wavered, but his motions were sure, disguising his inner turmoil. As he watched the group of stragglers meander toward the vehicles, Clay considered the fact that those rescued over the last twenty-four hours might now be an elite group of survivors, no longer misfits that were left behind. He knew he had to get them away from that energy field and out of the open, where they seemed like fresh meat for the virus-impaired crazed.

Alayna guided her patrol car back toward town, Clay and Daniels following close behind. They sped through the deserted streets, continuing to disobey common traffic laws. Clay and Brandon didn’t have words for each other. What they’d just seen was treacherous, dramatic—but certainly not as horrible as Brittany’s death earlier in the afternoon. Clay couldn’t bring himself to think about Valarie and Maia, hopefully tucked away safely in Austin. He felt the weight of his phone in his pocket, remembering that the cell phone towers were no longer operable. He just wished he could talk to them—hear their comforting voices. But he was alone, isolated. He and his group of survivors had nothing but each other.

The three vehicles parked outside the hotel, finding crooked spots on Main Street. The group rushed into the hotel, breathing heavily. Ralph stomped directly up the steps and toward the bar. His unsteady hands wrapped around a large bottle of bourbon, and he tilted it back quickly. Clay watched him from the corner, inhaling sharply, sure the man would lurch forward, vomiting.

Finally, Daniels reached forward and snuck the bottle away from Ralph, leaving the man gasping. No one spoke. They turned toward Clay, assessing their leader. He could sense their thoughts. *What the hell were they going to do?*

He swiped his hand over his balding head and eyed the clock. His mind was pulsing with fear, and he couldn't calculate how much time they had left. Whatever it was, it didn't seem like enough.

"We don't have a way to contact the government," Clay finally spoke, realizing honesty was essential. "The cell towers are down. And our walkie-talkies simply won't reach that far. Without Lieutenant Daniels's device to get us out . . ." His words drifted off.

Daniels took a hearty sip of the bourbon and swiped the back of his hand across his mouth with a violent motion. "He's right. But do we even want to get out of here?" he said gruffly. "Whatever those things are out there, they are just as rampant as the ones that were inside the containment zone. There's no telling which is the safer play."

Norah collapsed onto a barstool, her white, permed hair lopsided on her head. She clacked her knuckles against the bar counter, and Ralph handed her an entire liter of vodka. She uncapped it with a flourish and sipped from the bottle. It was clear: she felt she was nearing the end of her life after a long, hard road.

"Whatever," Brandon scoffed, sitting next to Norah and pouring himself a glass from her bottle. "Maybe we should all just give up and die. It's not like we have a lot to live for anymore."

The air was tense with low morale. Everyone except Daniels, Alayna, and Clay seemed to drink quickly, allowing the comfort of alcohol to fold over them. Clay felt too guilty to drink and too tense to eat. His stomach flipped as he eyed Alayna. With her hands stuffed in her pockets and her nose toward the ground, she looked defeated, a shell of her former self.

"I just wanted to find her," she whispered. "You don't think she went toward the energy field, do you?"

"We can't know anything," Clay said. "We didn't see any sign of her. It's no good to think the worst. Hope is the only thing we have."

"And we don't have a whole lot of it," Brandon blurted, tilting his head back for another sip. "Hope won't bring back my sister or my parents. I'm alone now, without anyone to call my own."

Clay didn't speak. Brandon's snide tone cut through him. Beside him, Daniels leaned toward Alayna, sadness in his eyes. "You know, Alayna," he began, "I'm really sorry for everything that happened. I mean, how I treated you. Not listening to you. And then—and then becoming a part of you and Megan's fight—" He paused, his voice haggard. "I didn't mean for this to come out of it."

Alayna turned away from him, blinking wildly, hiding tears. "Whatever, Lieutenant. You cocky bastard. You thought you could save us all. But all you did was ruin my life." Her voice was wistful, almost lost. She lifted a finger high in the air, gesturing toward Ralph. "Pour me one of those, will you?"

Ralph bowed his head, pouring the drink and sliding it across the countertop. Alayna wrapped her hands around it, sipping it with closed eyes. With that single motion, Clay felt her slipping away.

Suddenly, Clay noticed movement out the window. Something white flashed across the corner before darting out of sight. He rushed forward, pressing his nose close to the glass. "What the hell," he muttered.

"What is it?" Daniels asked, joining him.

There, in the center of Main Street, stood a tall, dark-haired man wearing a long white medical coat. He held his chin high as he moved, walking in great strides with a sense of immediacy.

"Who's that?" Daniels asked, eyeing Clay. "You know everyone in this town, don't you?"

Clay shook his head, trying to get a better look at the man's face. "He's a stranger."

"I thought you swept the town clean?" Brandon asked.

Clay turned from the window, questions running through his mind. He charged toward the staircase, Daniels hot on his heels. Who was this mysterious man wandering through Carterville?

52.

Clay and Daniels bounded from the hotel and ran down Main Street and toward the white-coated man. The moment their boots hit the pavement, the man heard them and began to run, his coat streaming behind him like a cape.

"HEY! WE'RE NOT THEM!" Clay cried. "WE WANT TO HELP!"

Daniels grunted. "I don't think he thinks we're going to eat him. He's avoiding us for some other reason. Come on. He's fast."

They bolted down Main Street, past the toy store and the church. Clay's lack of sustenance made his limbs quake. He stretched his legs farther, watching as Daniels skirted ahead of him, chasing after the mystery man. He watched as the white coat turned at Moe's Candy and bounded up the steps.

Clay and Daniels reached the entrance right before the white-coated man tried to lock the door. Beneath his dark hair, he wore a panicked expression, assuring Clay that something was amiss. In this desolate scenario, why would anyone run from a sheriff?

The man began to back through the candy store, busting his elbow against various containers. Gumballs and licorice and chocolate balls scattered to the ground. A smile stretched across his face, showing bright white teeth—so strange and stark amid all the candy.

"Stop right there," Clay ordered. "We're just here to save you. You have nowhere to run."

The man's eyebrows rose high. He took another step backward, knocking into a large jar of jelly beans. They spilled to the floor, raining oranges and reds and yellows. "You don't know what you're talking about," the man whispered, His voice ominous.

Daniels lunged forward, reaching toward the tall, lanky man. Just as his firm fingers wrapped around the man's upper arm, the man reached behind him, grasping at what appeared to be a hidden door. He lunged against Daniels's grasp, huffing. "Let go of me," he protested.

"WHO THE HELL ARE YOU?" Daniels blared, shaking him. "Didn't you get the evacuation notice? Don't you know you shouldn't be here?"

Clay stood beside him, then, glaring at the stranger. "We don't want to hurt you. Just tell us what you're running from. Why are you here? What's going on?"

The man bolted back toward the door again, grabbing a large jar of jawbreakers and throwing it at his pursuers. It smashed against Daniels's face. He surged for the door again and rushed into the darkness. After a split second of panic, Daniels yanked him back into the light and punched him, first in the stomach and then across his temple. The man skidded back, flailing against the store shelves and shattering more jars of candy. His eyes closed, and he fell from consciousness.

Clay gripped Daniels's arm, flustered. "Why the hell did you do that?" he cried.

"What do you mean?" Daniels asked, incredulous.

"Why'd you punch him? Why'd you knock him out? You had him in your grasp," Clay said, scoffing.

"I don't know what the big deal is. We got him, didn't we?"

"Sure. But he's still civilized," Clay said, gesturing to the man slumped on the ground. "This guy, he wasn't showing signs of the crazed. I don't think he was going to eat us or anything."

"But he was up to something, or why would he run and put up a fight?" Daniels said, shrugging. He lifted the man up by his armpits before flinging him over his shoulder.

"Well, that's not the tactic I would have used," Clay sighed, eyeing the devastation of the candy store.

"He's nothing but a schmuck, Clay. Let's get him back to the hotel and wait for him to wake up there. Then we question the hell out of him."

Daniels retreated from Moe's Candy and began to retrace his steps, the body of the white-coated man flapping against his back.

53.

Daniels carried the unconscious man up the steps and into the hotel bar, where the other survivors awaited them, sipping languidly from their drinks. The moment Clay appeared, Alayna stirred. She knocked the rest of her drink back before slurring, "Who's that?"

"Don't know," Daniels offered, dropping the man into a chair at the center of the room. "We should tie him up."

"Tie him up?" Alayna asked. "What do you mean? Why is he unconscious?"

"It'd take too long to explain," Daniels said gruffly. "This one's sour. That's all you need to know."

Alayna searched Clay's face, her lips parting with confusion.

"But he's left behind, just like all of us," Ralph mumbled. "What we should do is get him a room to sleep it off."

"He assaulted us and tried to flee," Clay said, reaching for several towels draped across the bar. He wrapped them around the man's wrists, tying him to the wooden chair. "We need to talk to him before anything else."

"Jesus," Brandon scoffed. "What kind of loonies are you?"

Clay poured a large glass of water, sipped a bit

from the top, and then tossed the rest over the unconscious man's face. After a second, he began to sputter and cough, finding consciousness again. He blinked rapidly, assessing his surroundings.

"Who are you?" Clay asked him, his voice stern.

The man coughed again, stomping his feet on the ground, realizing he was tied. "Get me out of here!" he cried.

"Who are you?" Clay asked again, leaning toward him, his face mere inches away from the stranger's.

"I don't understand. I haven't done anything wrong," the man spat. He'd looked strong, dominant, and tall during his rush toward the candy store. But now he looked weak, like a child. "Let me go."

"Listen here," Clay said, his eyes flashing. "I've been a sheriff here for nearly fifteen years. Which means I know just about everyone here in Carterville. And guess what? I don't know you. I don't recognize your face."

"What of it?" the man said.

"Tell me your name. Tell me who you are and why you ran. And then, maybe, I can consider letting you free."

The man sighed, his eyes glancing toward the door. After a moment of brimming silence, he answered. "My name is Leland Jacobs. You don't know me because I've only just moved here. For a job."

Clay scoffed. "For a job. I'm assuming that's selling sweets, then? Because you sure as hell don't look like you belong in a candy store." He assessed him, turning his eyes from his white shoes to the top of his gleaming forehead. "You're dressed more like a scientist than anything. But we don't keep your stock around here in Carterville."

The man smiled, showing those bright, ominous teeth again.

"Yeah. Come to think of it, you don't look like anyone I've seen around here, either," Ralph said, coming out from around the bar. He stumbled but caught himself before falling to the ground. "And I've lived here my entire life."

"Never seen him either," Norah said, her eyebrows slanting.

"Tell us the truth, Leland," Clay said, leaning even closer. His eyes penetrated Leland's, causing the intensity to mount.

"Like you said, I work at Moe's. My name is Leland Jacobs. And I've only just moved here," the man said, brimming with confidence. "That's about as much as I can tell you. Just like you, I am a simple man with simple habits."

Clay crossed his arms over his chest and made momentary eye contact with Daniels, who made a slashing motion across his neck. It was clear this man wasn't telling the truth. But why in the world would he be lying? Again, his gut felt stretched, giving him the sense that something was amiss. The Carterville he'd grown to know and love wouldn't host someone like this. Leland Jacobs was surely a fraud. But how could he get to the bottom of it?

54.

Suddenly Daniels reached forward, grasping Leland's forearm with tight fingers. The skin surrounding his grasp turned pale white and Leland's eyes closed with pain.

"You're going to tell us the truth now, Leland," Daniels said coldly. "We're done fucking around. You understand?"

Clay took a step forward. The tension in the room was palpable. "That'll be enough, Lieutenant."

But Daniels pressed on, ignoring Clay's order.

"There's . . . nothing . . . to tell," Leland winced in pain. "I have nothing to tell you."

These words fueled Daniels, causing him to untie the towels from the man's wrist and lift him into the air once more. Anger made his muscles writhe. He began to stretch Leland's arm behind his back, twisting it. Beside Clay, Norah placed her fingers over her mouth in horror.

"Jesus," Alayna gasped. But still, Daniels stretched the arm back farther. Leland's face drained of color. He looked moments from passing out. He began to squeal with pain, the noise echoing off the walls.

Brandon ran from the room, storming down the hallway. He slammed a door, clearly frustrated. But Ralph egged Daniels on. "We don't have time for this.

Break his arm! He's a coward and a criminal."

Suddenly Alayna burst forward, wrapping her hand around Daniels's massive arm, shaking her head. "Stop, Adam," she whispered, her voice like a lover's. "Please."

Daniels's grip immediately loosened. Leland closed his mouth, halting his scream. Alayna peered at him with calm eyes. "It's clear that he's hiding something, but torture is not the way. Not today," she said. "Maybe we isolate him in a room while we work some things out. We can't be rash." She gave both Clay and Daniels a dark look, causing Clay's stomach to flip. His anger receded evenly. "Both of you should know that," she said firmly.

"I'll take him," Clay said, stepping forward and grasping Jacobs's arms, pulling them lightly behind his back. Something about Alayna's words remained in his mind, spinning, causing him endless shame. Always he and Alayna had been united. Did she see him on the other side, with Daniels? He hated the prospect.

"And if there's one, there might be more," Daniels said, eyeing Jacobs with a sideways glance.

Clay nodded reluctantly. "Agreed," he said, regaining his composure with every passing minute. "After Mr. Jacobs here is tucked away, let's go back out there and see if there are any more." Clay watched as Alayna's expression changed ever so slightly. It wasn't anything perceptible to the others in the group, but it was enough for him to notice.

Clay led Jacobs down the hall to the farthest room, stumbling lightly as he tried to keep the man upright. "I'm not sure what your real story is," he said, his voice harsh, "but I don't think you fully grasp what's at stake here."

"Enlighten me, then." Jacobs said. "You're leaving me in the dark here."

Clay's words came quickly. "In just a few hours, a chemical bomb will go off, with the potential to destroy us all. There's a security perimeter set up around the entire town, and we have no way out. One of the rescued citizens took the device that was our only way of deactivating the perimeter and then disappeared. Now we're trapped."

"You mean we're trapped here?" Jacobs asked, his voice rising high.

Clay loosened his grip, sensing Jacobs's question was weighted. Did he know something? He didn't respond, allowing silence to stretch between them. Down the hallway, Clay heard the survivors collapse at the bar, exhausted, requesting refills.

Clay and Jacobs reached the door, and Clay led them into the musty hotel room, crossing his thick forearms across his chest. Jacobs assessed him quietly. "How are your symptoms, anyway?" he asked coyly.

With a quick motion, Clay whisked his palm over the top of his head, feeling the coolness of his scalp through his thinning hair. "You noticed?" he whispered, incredulous. "I—I haven't felt exactly right since—"

Jacobs nodded, keeping his eyes focused. "Of course I noticed. I'm not blind."

Clay's voice became hushed. He closed the door halfway, eyeing his captive with suspicion. "It was vomiting and shivers and sweating at first. But now that seems to have ceased. I've been losing hair like crazy, sure. And my color must not be quite right."

Jacobs didn't speak for a moment, tracing his eyes down Clay's face and upper chest. When he spoke, he didn't offer an opinion.

"Do the others know, or are you deceiving them unfairly? Jacobs asked.

Clay felt smacked. He turned his eyes toward the ground, his arms hanging loosely. Why did he suddenly feel that Jacobs was questioning him now? He was ignorant, lost, the sad leader of a troop of survivors.

"Tell me more about this device," Jacobs said after a pause. "Listen, I can't tell you everything, but I can tell you that the device must be found. When was the last time it was seen?"

Clay shook his head. With a quick step back, he said, "That's quid pro quo" and then flung the door shut in Jacobs's face. He stood huffing, his eyes wide and bleary. Still, he sensed that Jacobs was still standing on the other side of the door glaring toward him, waiting for his response.

What on earth did this man know?

55.

Daniels marched down Main Street while Clay eyed the horizon. Their final inspection passed without speaking. It felt as if the town of Carterville had always been this barren—that the world he'd once inhabited had never truly existed. It was all a fantasy. Something for his mind to cling to for its own survival.

They'd scoured the final section of houses over the previous few hours, hardly discussing their next move and not mentioning the futility of it all. Without the device they felt useless, dead. Their wandering, searching for Megan and any other survivors, was an excuse to get them out of the hotel, where depression had cloaked everyone. The future felt grim.

They arrived back to the hotel and slogged through the door, Clay tapping his toe against the doorframe. Caked mud dropped on the once-fine and gleaming foyer floor. Upstairs, music boomed from the bar, a jangling tune that made Clay suspect it had been Ralph who'd chosen it. He'd lost his wife, and he was acting reckless, seeing nothing as human or real any longer.

Clay couldn't blame him.

Daniels and Clay climbed the steps, entering the bar to find Alayna, Brandon, Norah, and Ralph leaning sloppily on barstools, each with a drink in hand. Alayna's eyes glittered as Clay entered, happy for the familiar face.

"How'd it go out there? Did you find her?" she murmured as he passed. Her breath smelled of whiskey.

Clay allowed a stiff smile to form on his face. Morale was low, achingly so, but he needed to remain positive. "Nothing. No sign of Megan or anyone else for that matter. Probably means everyone else paid attention to the warnings. Good news, really."

Brandon scoffed, shooting some tequila down his throat. "Or they've been eaten by those monsters. Just like Brittany."

Clay and Alayna made eye contact. A small tear formed before rolling down her cheek. "Something happened," she said. Norah placed her palm on Alayna's back, rubbing at the tense muscles.

"What is it?" he asked. He felt his heart rise in his chest. "It wasn't Leland, was it? I locked the door—"

Alayna shook her head. "Ralph went in to check on Dr. Miller. But he passed."

With all the madness, Clay had nearly forgotten the sick doctor, stuck away in that sour-smelling hotel room. He pressed his lips together, understanding the dismal morale now, and almost embracing it. His chest constricted. He collapsed beside Alayna, sick with the knowledge that they'd lost another one. Then a sudden fear overtook him. "Did he—"

Alayna shook her head. "There was nothing we could do," Alayna said. "He died in peace and was completely still when we found him."

"We took care of it," Ralph said, a burp erupting from between his lips. He staggered forward, his steps sloppy. "Didn't want him polluting the rest of us, or decaying. So we wrapped him in plastic and put him downstairs. In the big freezer."

The image of that emaciated, faded man slumped over in the freezer, waiting to be buried, chilled Clay to the bone.

"It was the only thing we could think to do," Alayna said. "Till you got back."

Clay nodded. He leaned forward, wrapping his fingers around the whiskey bottle, and then tilted the bottle to his lips. The liquid burned as it went down. Hunger pangs filled him, strange in the place of such sadness and desolation. As he continued to sip, fear of the unknown pulsed through him. The jangling country album finished, and deadly silence began. Norah finished her drink and hung her head sadly. Her wrinkles looked deeper, pushing her eyes far back in her skull. She's lived a long life, Clay thought.

After several minutes of silence, Ralph smacked his palm against the counter, momentarily energetic. "Fuck it," he scoffed. "Fuck all of this. I say we go down and cook up some of those amazing steaks we just saw in the freezer. Cook up whatever we can find in the kitchen, for tonight. Goodness knows we all need a meal. We've been sustaining ourselves on nothing but the drink for days, it seems."

"Will it really matter?" Brandon said. "We'll all die tomorrow." His sarcasm pulled the morale down another notch.

But Norah lifted herself from the stool, wiping her fingers across her dress. "I'll go down, take the steaks out, and get some water boiling for a side." Her limbs creaked, but she moved swiftly, descending the steps with Ralph following lazily. Somehow this motion to feed everyone—even if it was the last thing they did—rejuvenated them. Gave them purpose. "Come on, Brandon. You're part of us now. You're gonna learn to cook," Norah said as she disappeared through the doorway.

Clay shrugged languidly at Alayna, who placed a secret hand upon his knee—a reminder of the once-comfortable life they'd shared at the station. "You want to grab another drink?" she said, eyeing Daniels, who stood near the window. "Both of you?"

Daniels agreed heartily, taking quick steps toward the bar and pouring them each doubles of whiskey. "We better die soon," he scoffed, a strange smile stretching across his face. "Otherwise, we'll run out of booze and start killing each other."

56.

In the kitchen, Norah began to order Brandon and Ralph, noting that both were sloppy drunk and staggering into pots and pans, their elbows flailing. "Why don't you men learn to control yourselves?" she bellowed, thinking back to her old days at the library, when she'd spent hours alone, wandering through shelves. She'd kill for that kind of solitude now.

"Let's organize this kitchen before we get started," she said, rubbing her wrinkled hands together. "Brandon, grab that big pot over there, fill it with water, and bring it to a boil. I found a large vat of pasta in the pantry, and I think it would be a nice side."

"We got sauce?" Ralph asked, eyeing her wearily. "I won't eat it without sauce."

Norah stifled an eye roll. In all her years at the library, she hadn't seen Ralph pass through the shelves, questing for knowledge. Surely he'd spent much of his days with that sour woman, his now-deceased wife, wasting time at the bar.

But the time for judgment was now over.

Norah passed the freezer, shivering, remembering the way Dr. Miller's body had hung, lazily, dripping from his sores, as Ralph and Brandon had carried him to the freezer. Her stomach had churned, reminding her of her experience reading countless adventure or apocalyptic books. Always the hero had found a way to push through to the end. But they lost so many stragglers along the way.

And what kind of irony was it that the very man who'd stayed behind to keep them alive was now dead in their freezer?

"Ralph, would you mind getting the steaks?" she asked lightly.

Ralph marched forward like an army private following his general's orders. But as he placed his hand upon the freezer door handle, the three of them heard an unmistakable thud coming from inside.

"The hell?" Brandon cried, dropping a pan on the floor. It whirled around, clanking against the tile. The three of them stood staring.

"Do you think he's still alive?" Ralph rasped. "Can't be. We all checked his pulse. Right?"

No one spoke. In the moments that followed, the banging picked up again, but with more intensity.

"We shouldn't open it," Brandon said quickly. "We should just go upstairs. Keep drinking. This is stupid, anyway."

"What are you talking about?" Ralph cried. "We put a man in there. If he's alive, we need to get him out. He'll freeze to death."

Norah cupped her hands together, her eyelids fluttering. This was a nightmare. She would wake up soon, wrapped in her blankets, with the sun spilling in through the open window.

Ralph eased forward and flung open the freezer door. There, at the far side of the freezer, leaning against the wall, was Dr. Willis Miller—the very man they'd covered in plastic and laid to rest. But he was standing. And he was banging his head against the galvanized metal surface, purple spurts of blood oozing from his ears, the plastic tarp rumpled at his feet. Terrified, Norah jumped back. The sound of his head splattering filled her with agony.

"What the shit?" Ralph said, still holding on to the freezer door, glaring. "What's gotten into him?"

As his words echoed throughout the kitchen, the figure in the freezer stopped his manic self-defacing and suddenly burst toward Ralph, his eyes crazed. His nose oozed something unrecognizable and his eyes were sunk far in his shattered skull. An eerie smile crept across his face, showing blackening teeth.

Ralph began to shut the door in a panic, yelling. But Dr. Miller thrust his hand through the opening, ensuring that the latch didn't engage. Ralph wasn't quick enough. The doctor lunged from the door, pushing Ralph onto his back and smashing into a pile of dishes.

Norah acted quickly. Her lithe fingers wrapped around a skillet, and she flung it at Dr. Miller's skull, gashing him directly above his eyes. He turned toward her, angry screams bursting from his wide mouth. Norah backed through the kitchen, waiting, accepting her end. She watched the kitchen light gleam against the monster's glistening blood. She should have died in some sad, beeping hospital, surrounded by silly plants and Get Well Soon cards.

But the dead man was too dilapidated to get far. His leg, which had begun to mold during his stint in bed, gave out under him, and his body crashed to the ground. His flailing arms thrashed against a stack of dishes. The white saucers shattered across the floor, crashing into Brandon and Norah's shoes.

The monster didn't quit. He scrambled to his hands and knees and began to crawl toward

Brandon, his tongue lolling from his mouth. Brandon backed wildly into a corner, waving a skillet in the air. "GET AWAY FROM ME. GET BACK," he screamed, tears rolling down his face. As the monster crawled, splinters from the white plates sliced his hands, coating the floor in his poisoned blood.

But just before the dead man reached Brandon, Clay burst in, his gun held high. He brushed past Norah and launched two bullets directly into Dr. Miller's skull, splattering blood across the sinks and wall. The body, nearly headless, flung across the floor, lifeless.

Alayna and Daniels rushed into the room right behind Clay. Brandon sputtered with panic in the corner, and Norah joined Ralph still lying on the floor, suddenly feeling closer to him after the terrible encounter. They all looked at Clay with large, childlike eyes.

Clay shoved his gun back into his holster, sweat pouring down his face. "Shall we find something else to eat, then?" he said, and Norah was surprised at the strength of his voice. "I think steaks might be out for now."

57.

In the short time that followed, Clay, Alayna, and Daniels rewrapped the plastic around Dr. Miller's body and lowered him into a shallow grave Daniels had dug almost two miles away from the hotel. As they entombed the doctor, Ralph, Norah, and Brandon undertook the terrible burden of cleaning the kitchen, scrubbing the bloody floors and walls silently, with even Ralph unable to find words. Despite their different backgrounds, the remaining survivors ached with a similar, silent melancholy.

Norah prepared a massive pot of steaming pasta and a seasoned marinara sauce. Brandon found some bread and sprinkled it with garlic and cheeses, creating his once-favorite treat. The survivors no longer felt hunger in the traditional sense. Rather, they ached with an emptiness that extended down to their toes.

At around midnight, Daniels soldiered up the steps with a massive dining room table, placing it in the center of the bar room. He brushed his hands over his pants, shrugging toward Alayna. "I found some linen tablecloths downstairs. You think we should—"

Alayna nodded silently. She followed him, collecting the tablecloths, several candles, silverware, and plates and creating a prim and proper table—fit for a Thanksgiving dinner. Norah looked on with approval, her eyes catching the light of the candles. "If only we had flowers," she said, drifting her hand down Alayna's back. "Imagine how beautiful."

"As usual, I suppose, we'll have to make due," Alayna whispered.

The remaining survivors—excluding Leland Jacobs, locked away in his hotel room—gathered around the table and held hands in a tight circle, gazing at each other incredulously and allowing the dinner smells to course over them. Clay searched for the proper words to say. Perhaps a prayer? he thought. But in the moments that followed, he collapsed into his chair, and the others followed suit. He couldn't possibly make this okay.

They ate quickly and quietly, gobbling strings of spaghetti and spinning their forks through the sauce. Clay eyed Norah, sensing a slight twinge of pride within her. This was a glorious, fulfilling meal, already bringing life to the survivors' cheeks.

With a final flourish, Clay swiped a piece of bread over the last bit of sauce from his third helping before rising from his chair and creeping down the hallway, centered on his plan. As he moved, he felt thankful for each breath, for the blood that pumped through him. What a miracle it all was, he thought. He supposed everyone thought that in the end.

He opened Jacobs's door to find him leaning stiffly against the wall, his knees bent, but his face firm and docile. Clay gestured toward the hallway. "Come out, Leland," he said. This was his peace offering. It was all going to end soon anyway.

Leland didn't speak. He followed Clay into the dining room, where the other survivors surveyed him with suspicion.

"You didn't handcuff him?" Daniels asked, his eyebrows lowering. "We can't trust him, Clay."

Clay shrugged lightly, eyeing Jacobs, who looked like no monster with his lanky arms and dark eyes. "Adam, it's the end. We're all going to die in a matter of hours. All of us. And I don't think Leland's last night on earth should be spent alone."

No one spoke. Norah creaked from her chair and filled a plate for Jacobs, setting it at an open seat and pouring him a glass of wine. "Come on, honey," she said. "Eat up. You must be starved."

Leland sat primly at the edge of the chair, clearly conscious of everyone's eyes upon him. He thanked them, his eyes far away, and then he gratefully stuffed a large bite of spaghetti into his mouth. Somehow, with this very human act, the room warmed to him.

"I'm going to play a record," Ralph said, pushing away from the table and walking to the vinyl collection at the far wall. He slipped an old Johnny Cash record onto the turntable. When he returned to the table, tears were rolling down his cheeks. "This was Connie's favorite album. Strange to think that tonight will be the last time I ever hear it."

"We can play it all night long," Norah said, giving him a smile.

Daniels retrieved several more bottles of wine and began to refill everyone. Clay gazed at his comrades, the final people of his life, and images of his wife and daughter flashed through his mind. He'd had so much hope for Maia's future. And he'd loved Valerie as best as he'd been able to since he'd first seen her as a teenager. With his eyelashes fluttering against his cheeks, he thanked the wide universe for those gifts. And he quietly gave them up, understanding that he could no longer have such happiness or such freedom ever again.

58.

Hours later, the survivors drunkenly stumbled to their individual rooms. As they walked, Leland smacked a friendly palm against Clay's back, nodding firmly. "Thank you for that," he said, his eyes far away. "I needed it."

Clay nodded silently as he stepped into his room and closed his bedroom door. His ears still rang with Johnny Cash tunes. He collapsed upon his bed, fully clothed, his legs stretched out in front of him. He drummed his fingers against his taut stomach, trying to force the room to stop spinning.

Suddenly a knock came from the door. Clay cleared his throat, calling out, "Come in!"

Alayna appeared in the soft light from the hallway. Her black hair coursed down her shoulders and back, making her face look youthful and rather pretty, even with the slight mascara caked around her eyes from crying. "Mind if I come in?" she asked.

"Course not," Clay said, beckoning. He rose up, leaning heavily against the bed's backboard. Alayna sat next to him, staring at her kicking feet. "Quite a night we've had, huh?" Clay offered.

"Quite a night," Alayna agreed. "I—I just don't want to be alone."

Clay felt the depth of her sadness. He reached for her shoulder, kneading at her tense muscles. "I know. Neither do I," he said. "Too many thoughts to think. Too many memories."

"Tons of memories from our time together," Alayna agreed, smiling sadly. "I still remember my first day as your deputy. I was so frightened of you, until you took that bite of your burger."

"And got mayonnaise all over my uniform. Yep. I remember," Clay said, shocked at how easy his laughter came. "I couldn't pretend to be any kind of big shot around you after that."

Alayna smiled. "I was so confused about everything. But not about my career. I felt at home with you. I don't know if that makes sense." She looked at him, her vibrant, youthful body brimming with sexuality. Clay turned toward the window, alarmed by his sudden attraction to her. But he kept up the conversation, not wanting her to return to the hall.

"I know what you mean," Clay said, sensing them ebbing toward unknown territory. "You were my work wife for all those years. I couldn't have imagined having anyone else on the force."

"A work wife?" Alayna said, giggling. "That's such a sexist remark." She smacked her palm lightly against his shoulder.

The moment he felt her touch, his pulse quickened. What was going on?

"I didn't mean to offend," Clay said. "I mean, all bets are off here, right? I've grown to care about you like family. You must know this."

Alayna didn't speak for a moment. The silence held between them. Clay swallowed, wondering if he'd crossed some kind of line. His drunken words had surely given her pause.

But Alayna tried to bridge the gap, to lighten the

mood. She swiped at her tears. “Daniels tried to hit on me. What a bum, you know? But you know what I told him? I told him that I wouldn’t be with him if he was the last man on earth. It feels rather fitting, now,” she said, grinning. Suddenly, her eyes turned to Clay’s again. She lifted her face. “I don’t know how I would have reacted if it had been you. Probably very, very differently.”

Clay’s lips parted. In a moment of passion, he leaned toward her—his deputy, one of his best friends—and kissed her fully, wrapping his lips around her large bottom one. His head spun with the pleasure of it. Alayna’s scent coursed through his nose, making his groin stir.

Seconds later, he broke the kiss. “I can’t,” he said, wiping his fingers over his mouth. “I’ve never been unfaithful to Valerie. I’ve never even been with anyone else. Sure, I’ve always found you attractive. But I’ve never, in my wildest dreams, considered acting upon those feelings.”

Alayna tilted her head and lifted her hand to his cheek, stroking his grizzled cheek. He eyed her breasts, rising and falling beneath her white undershirt. “But Clay,” she whispered, “I’m the last woman on earth. And tomorrow, none of this will matter. We’ll all be dust tomorrow.”

Clay contemplated her words for a long time. Finally, he dove into her. He wrapped his arms around her, clinging to her, and kissed her fully, without looking back. They became a flurry of wild limbs, tossing clothes to the floor and fulfilling a destiny they’d never really imagined. Clay felt the warmth and smoothness of her skin as he unsnapped her bra. Thoughts of the outside world or of their impending doom no longer filled him. Rather, his mind and body and spirit were fueled with thoughts of Alayna only.

They made love deep into the night.

59.

When Clay awoke, Alayna wasn't in his bed. He stretched out beneath the sheets, feeling his bones creaking, remembering how wonderful it had been to coil himself around her warmth, to listen to her breathing as she fell into sleep. The feeling didn't last, though. Waves of regret plummeted through his mind.

With a jolt, he remembered this was the last day of his life. He dropped his feet to the frigid ground, dressed, and opened his door, listening. Down the hallway, at the bar, he caught images of several of the survivors, holding pots and pans and speaking amicably.

He joined them, noting that he was the last of the party to awake. Alayna sat at the edge of the bar holding a mug of coffee. She gave him a sideways smile, looking sheepish. Norah had cooked several omelets, a large vat of breakfast potatoes, and sausages, and someone had set the table again: a reminder that, for these hours only, they were still human. They could still appreciate beautiful things.

Alayna sat across the table from him. She eased her foot along his beneath the table, unbeknownst to anyone else. This was their secret, their first and final affair.

"Let's eat," Daniels said, diving into the bowl of

potatoes and filling his plate. The others followed suit, eating heartily without speaking. Their final sustenance was salty and greasy and good, filling Clay's hungover stomach and making him feel whole again.

As their forks and knives began to clink back to their plates, Jacobs cleared his throat, wiping his napkin over his lips. His eyes were dark, ominous. "I have something to say," he began.

Clay turned toward him, curious. "What is it?" he asked, standing as the spokesperson for the wide-eyed crew of survivors. "Whatever it is, you can tell us."

Jacobs sighed heavily, splaying his palms on the table. After a brief hesitation, he began. "I'm the cause of all of this," he said.

"But, the meteor—" Norah gasped.

Jacobs shook his head, interrupting. "No. Norah, I'm sorry. Just let me finish."

Clay was frozen, his emotions in turmoil. He couldn't feel anger. It wouldn't be worthwhile. He wanted to think of Valerie, and what a beautiful life they'd had together, but all he could think of was the passion he and Alayna had shared last night. He knew he should feel terrible, but in the end, he just wanted to feel.

"You said you wanted to know who I am. Well, I'm a scientific researcher contracted by the Department of Defense. I'm involved in the creation and development of nanite technology for the military. Carterville was chosen as one of the locations for this development. I can't say why. I wasn't involved in that decision.

"The research and experimentation was, initially, going quite well. We hoped to inject nanites into human hosts, with the intent of giving humans higher strength, above-average mental aptitude, and increased stamina. All things you'd expect and want in a soldier, yes?"

No one answered him. He had the floor. The air was electric with the others' focus on his words.

"Throughout the experiment, the nanites continued to die off after a very short period, after around forty-eight hours. This was not the desired effect. Extending their lifetimes was dangerous. But of course, in the interest of science and research, we wanted to push their effectiveness and activity period. It was one of the higher-up's idea to have the nanites learn to replicate themselves, thus extending the duration of their effectiveness.

"At first the experimentation had resounding success. But then, something changed. The nanites became autonomous and started taking over the human host, until the takeover was irreversible. You see, once the nanites have a human host, they can continue to survive indefinitely. The next step in their evolution was that they figured out a way to jump from host to host. They're really quite extraordinary, almost intelligent. And . . . the only way to stop them is by ceasing all brain activity in the host."

Clay remembered the moment that he'd lifted his gun to Cliff Henderson's crazed head, blasting grey matter across the jail cell wall. He shivered. It felt like a million lifetimes ago.

"As you've probably seen, once the nanites mutate, they create psychotic behavior in their hosts."

"The people who attacked my sister?" Brandon breathed, his face calm, accepting the words. Everyone else remained silent, allowing the truth to unfold before them. It was far more horrifying than they'd initially thought. It was purposeful.

"She died?" Jacobs asked.

Brandon nodded almost imperceptibly. "She was mauled by those . . . monsters. Just like my parents were."

"I'm afraid so," Jacobs continued, bowing his head. "And the meteorite? That was just a fluke. A lucky, cosmic event that allowed us to hide what was truly going on. In the end, we were able to evacuate the city without divulging the nature of the DOD project. How about that." He dropped his hands into his lap, clearly irritated, wanting the story to be over. But he continued.

"When I signed on for this job, I knew the risks involved. I did. I knew this could happen—although it was highly unlikely." He tilted his head, mulling over his words. "But here we are, with this outbreak ultimately contained inside the energy field. The fumigation that Colonel Wallace described is just a ruse. The solution is much more extreme. There's a neutralizing device that will go off, and the moment it does—in just a few hours—all living tissue in the containment zone will die. This way, the world outside will remain safe from this humanity-destroying catastrophe." He paused, finalizing his story. "So you see, we have to die here. But we're doing it so the rest of the world can live."

"But we saw them on the outside," Norah whispered. Her eyes traced toward Clay's. "Didn't we? We saw them. Outside the energy field?"

Clay nodded. The nightmarish recollection of the crazed rushing toward them from the burning, smoking vehicle on the highway before fizzling into blood and guts during their attack made him see red.

Clay scoffed, suddenly wishing he hadn't eaten so much breakfast. "Leland, it seems that your brilliant and reckless plan is far too late. It's too late for everyone, not just for us."

60.

"What do you mean, outside?" Jacobs asked, his voice coming harshly. "How could they?" He breathed heavily, his eyes dancing as he panicked, thinking. "The nanites simply can't be transferred from host to host by mere proximity alone. There would have to be some form of viral transfer. So it's rather unlikely that those people retrieved the nanites just by sitting next to someone." He eyed Clay, waiting for answers.

Clay leaned back heavily in his chair, remembering two days ago, when Alayna had been nothing but his deputy, when his daughter had complained about high school problems and the flu, when the world had carried along without a care.

"The first person I saw with symptoms like this was . . . Cliff. Cliff Henderson," Clay said. "And he was in the cell with Trudy." The realization struck him all at once. He felt he'd been punched in the gut.

"Henderson. Right," Jacobs repeated, his eyes assured. "He worked at the lab. He was part of the team."

Clay looked aghast. "He had kissed Trudy. They were both brought in couple nights ago."

Everyone at the table sighed heavily with the all-knowing, collective consciousness of a small town. "Shit. I can't believe Trudy was our downfall," Ralph said, his voice sarcastic.

"What is it about this Trudy woman?" Jacobs asked, incredulous. "So she kissed Cliff. You said she was in jail?"

"You don't understand," Norah said. "Trudy. She was a rather loose woman. The town floozy, if you will. Every town has one. And she was ours. I appreciated her for it. She always had a great story."

"And she was almost always in our jail for being drunk and disorderly," Alayna chimed in. "Just the way she reached toward people with those big, beautiful lips. She kissed me once, years ago. Threw me off for days." Alayna paused. "And she was released the morning Cliff went berserk."

No one spoke. Clay's stomach twisted, imagining a crazed, lunatic Trudy rambling through the world with purple and red pus pulsing from lesions on her arms and legs. He shivered, wishing he could remember her as the pretty, if messy and wild, girl he'd known so well. "Shit. She must have been the way it got outside. She is, or was, the source—beyond Cliff, that is."

"What about the farmer and his daughter?" Alayna asked. "After the meteorite. I noticed that they both had the sweats. They were out of it, clearly messed up. Weren't they infected?" She blinked wildly.

Jacobs shrugged. "It could be a number of things, really. Anything from the flu that's been running rampant to the effects of radiation exposure," he said, glancing at Clay. "If they were family, it's more likely that they have both had the same cold. It's rather unlikely that they were demonstrating nanite symptoms."

"So it was just a coincidence?" Alayna whispered.

"Stranger things have certainly happened," Clay said, tilting his head.

"Sounds messed up," Ralph cried from the corner. "So the town slut is going to destroy the world? Ha. Connie always said to stay away from her. I did. Kept my affairs elsewhere."

"Well, you owe your life to her, then," Brandon said, laughing humorlessly. "I mean, you owe her your life for the next few hours. Until we're nothing but dust."

Jacobs spoke over them, becoming the voice of reason—the only one with actual, scientific knowledge. "It's probably a coincidence, yes. Unless they interacted with someone who was infected, with their blood or saliva." He shrugged again. "There's really no way to know without interviewing them."

"So after you're infected, what is the incubation period?" Clay asked, his eyebrows furrowed, thinking of his own symptoms. It seemed rather unlikely, at this point, that he was infected himself. But his hair still fluttered to the ground as he walked, and his joints ached. Perhaps Jacobs had answers.

"Anywhere from sixty minutes up to eighteen hours," Jacobs answered. "There's really nothing specific about the timing. It's how the nanites react to the individual host that's different. As I've heard, your Dr. Miller didn't show the psychotic signs until much, much after he was attacked. Meaning we don't have many answers. We only know . . . well," he paused, turning back to Clay, "if what you're saying is true, and the nanites have escaped the perimeter, we can assume that the contamination is spreading . . . worldwide at this point. We can assume that the human race won't last in these conditions."

"Jesus!" Ralph exclaimed. "Around the globe

already?"

Jacobs nodded. "There have been multiple researches on how viruses can spread. Within a little more than three months, complete saturation will be achieved. And with the added features that we've programmed into the nanites, it's much more severe. The nanites are simply too powerful."

Clay sat with these words. He realized in that moment that he'd been perfectly fine with dying, as long as the rest of the world was allowed to live. He wanted his daughter to grow older. He yearned for his wife to smile, every single day of her life, into old age.

But the world was grim and dark, teeming with sickness. And even Alayna, sitting before him, with her dark eyes upon him, couldn't bring any level of happiness. Humanity was doomed.

61.

Clay stood and began to pace, his arms behind his back. He hated the feeling of being trapped. He searched his mind, hoping for a flicker of resolve.

"So, we're fucked," Brandon said, scooting his chair back and looking at them blankly. "The entire planet. It's over, friends. We did the best we could."

Alayna peered at Clay, knowing him well enough to sense when something was brewing. "Clay. What are you thinking?" she asked.

Clay turned toward her, his feet spread wide apart, his stance dominant. Even Daniels seemed in awe of him. "I say we deactivate the device," he said sternly.

"What? Impossible," Jacobs said, shaking his head. "Absolutely not."

"Why? The contamination is everywhere, both inside and outside the energy field, meaning there's nothing to be solved by allowing the device to destroy us." His mind revved, realizing that he had a few more hours or days or even months to live, if Jacobs would allow it. "It would give us the time we need to figure this out. To find our families and protect them."

Across the table, Alayna shifted in her chair, suddenly restless. But Clay ignored her, staring intently at Jacobs. "It's no use for us all to die. Don't you understand?"

Clay searched the faces of his other survivors. Ralph began to mutter to himself, confusion filling him. "Well, if we don't have to die today—" he began.

Norah sighed. "I think what Clay is saying makes sense," she said. "We've come too far to give up. We've fought through these last few days. There's nothing that says we can't continue to fight."

Brandon smacked his palm against the table, shaking it. "Whatever. I'm in if you guys are. Come on, Leland. Even you don't want to die today. I can see it in you."

Daniels erupted from his chair, popping his hands upon Jacobs's chair and jiggling it. "You hear that, buddy? We have the beginning of a plan. Come on, now! Do the right thing. Not like last time, when you decided to destroy all of humanity."

Clay turned to Alayna. She hadn't spoken. She leaned heavily upon her fist, and her face was nondescript.

"I agree," she finally said, nodding. "It's the right thing to do."

"Very well, then," Jacobs said, leaning back in his chair. "But before I tell you, know this. I'll have nothing to do with it. You're just extending the inevitability of our deaths, and it's reckless. I think you all know that. Maybe all of you except your optimistic sheriff, here."

Clay glowered.

"But I'm guessing you won't have time to get there anyway. So it doesn't really matter to me. I'll live out the remainder of my time here, relaxed, contemplating me existence. The rest of you will rush off to the clock tower—the very top." His eyes glinted as he looked at his watch. "And seems like you only have about twenty minutes at this point. Isn't that so, Clay?"

"Twenty minutes? We'll never have time." Norah bowed her head. The sight of it was disheartening for Clay. A sign that just another in his troop of survivors was open to giving up.

Ralph gave up, too. "Hell, I don't care if we live or die any longer," he said, stabbing a fork into one of the remaining sausages and taking a menacing bite. "I ain't cared since Connie died. You all run off and find this device, or whatever. I'm going to have me a morning whiskey." He lifted from his chair and poured yet another glass, watching as the liquid glugged into the glass.

But Clay, Daniels, Alayna, and Brandon leaped from their chairs and bounded down the steps, fresh with the knowledge that they could live—they could continue to exist, to play this terrible game—for just a little bit longer. Brandon's long, lanky teenage legs allowed him to run faster and stronger than the others. And Clay felt a moment of pride, watching this once-sarcastic and snarky individual race for his freedom, and his life.

62.

The clock tower was about a half-mile away, a bit off Main Street, and tucked against the old cathedral, which had been built more than a century ago. Clay had necessarily passed the clock tower countless times in his cruiser, hardly viewing its age-old beauty. Miraculously, he'd never been inside. The view, he'd been told, wasn't remarkable any longer, since many of the old buildings had been demolished to make way for the highway and the multiple gas stations.

They raced toward it, each of them breathing heavily. Clay had stabbing pains up and down his abdomen from the sprint. He hunched over, gasping for oxygen. A stone archway loomed above the entrance. "Jesus," he breathed, gazing up at the high clock tower.

"COME ON!" Daniels cried, rushing through the doors and turning toward the stone steps. Clay followed after Alayna and Daniels, with Brandon close behind him. The feeling of trepidation was palpable, and they no longer spoke, recognizing that even one wasted minute meant the end of their lives.

The staircase wound upward, making Clay's head spin. Just as he thought he might vomit, they burst onto the landing. One by one, each of them gasped, recognizing precisely what awaited them at the top.

In the center of the clock tower's dome was a large, black orb, connected to countless wires and circuits and blinking lights. To the left of the orb, a clock ticked back the minutes, alerting them that they had just four minutes to figure out how to deactivate the bomb.

Clay wiped his hand over his thin hair, marching around and around it, trying to make sense of the wires and lights. The others followed suit, knowing they needed to move quickly—but that one false move meant it could detonate anyway. The moments were fragile.

"Jesus. We should have made him come with us," Brandon finally spoke, breaking the silence. "We don't know what the fuck we're doing. He's the one who's the scientist."

"Damn it," Daniels said, growling. "Three minutes, guys. We have to do something. We have to try."

"Well are you going to be the one?" Brandon asked, laughing. "Because I don't want to be the one to choose what will kill us. I'd rather let it go."

Clay began to twiddle with a few of the wires, knowing he had to make a move; he had to be the one with the confidence and bravery to persevere. He remembered the movies he'd watched as a kid, when the bomb was always deactivated two seconds before it detonated. Surely something would come to him. Sweat beads poured from his forehead, dripping down his cheeks.

Suddenly Alayna cut forward, easing in front of him. Clay stepped back, too curious to ask questions. With two minutes remaining, Alayna clicked a switch to the left of the countdown clock. The moment she did it, Clay closed his eyes, sensing destruction.

But as he stood with his eyes closed, Daniels let out a mighty roar. Clay moved his fingers, testing to see if his body was still intact. His thoughts swam freely. He felt things. He existed. He blinked to see Daniels wrap his arms around Alayna and lift her high into the air, bouncing her and crying out. "YES. SHE DID IT."

"You flipped the switch, and it worked?" Clay asked, incredulous. "That was all?"

Alayna grinned nervously. Daniels lowered her, and she shrugged, gesturing toward the now-blank countdown clock. None of the lights were on; the bomb no longer beeped. It looked dead and lifeless.

"The simplicity of it all," Clay said, slipping Alayna's hair behind her ear, trying to preserve this special moment in time.

"That was some timing," Daniels joked behind her, noting the intimacy between the two of them. "Some timing indeed."

63.

Brandon led the way back down the steps, taking them two at a time. His shoulders shook with relief. When they reached the early afternoon light on the street, he wrapped Alayna in a hug, looking briefly like an overjoyed kid. “I know it doesn’t matter. I know we’re probably going to die anyway,” he said, his smile wide. “But that was one of the greatest things I’ve ever seen. Thank you, Alayna. We all owe our lives to you.”

Alayna returned the hug but pulled away awkwardly. “Easy, there, Brandon. All I did was flip a switch. Nothing terribly heroic about it,” she said modestly.

Brandon’s sincerity made Clay grin cautiously. He sensed they’d only just begun a long and burdensome road. And someday, maybe soon, Brandon would die. And maybe they’d all have to watch it.

“Let’s get back to the hotel,” Alayna said, patting Brandon on the back as she moved past him. “I want to see the look on Leland’s face when he realizes we’re going to survive. Glad he chose today of all days to tell us the truth about the nanites. He could have told us last night and given us a bit more time . . .” She trailed off, falling into stride beside Clay. “Perhaps he liked the drama of it all.”

"Well, he truly didn't know about the spread of the infection," Clay offered. "And he obviously doesn't care about us at all. Why would he? He's not a native. He arrived, what? Just a few months ago?"

"Didn't reap any of our neighborly kindness," Brandon joked, stabbing his elbow into Daniels's side. "Not like this gentleman right here."

Daniels shrugged. "Small town or not, with people I know, or not—I was assigned to save Carterville. Didn't expect to make any friends along the way." He eyed both Alayna and Clay with subtle affection. Clay wondered if the man had ever made a friend in his life.

They returned to the hotel to find Ralph seated beside the record player, watching the vinyl spin and spin with a glass of whiskey in his hand. He was already bleary eyed, clearly attempting to reach darkness before the world blacked out around him. But the moment he saw them, he jumped to his feet. "What happened? Is it over?" he asked, slurring.

"We turned it off," Brandon said, patting him on the shoulder. "We live another day, old man."

"Huh," Ralph said, pouring himself another glass. "Well, can't say I'm surprised. I can't be surprised anymore. It's just been one thing after another."

"Where's Norah?" Clay asked.

"She went to her room to lie down. Didn't want to see it happen," Ralph said. "And that Leland asshole, he's in his room, too. Said he was going to do some reading. I don't trust him." His white eyebrows furrowed deeply.

Jacobs appeared in the doorway, then, Norah following close behind. Norah's face was content, with a slight smile. She wrapped her arms around

Alayna, giving her a soft kiss on the cheek.

"You should be thanking her," Clay offered. "She's the one who flipped the switch."

"That's my girl," Norah said kindly, gliding her fingers over her hair. "I knew you all could do it. I just couldn't make it myself." She blinked softly.

But Jacobs scoffed, his forearms crossed over his chest. "Well, now what? We get to live another day," he affirmed. "But what about tomorrow? And what about the day after that? We're all dead already. And you know it."

"Sure. With an attitude like that, I suppose you're right," Clay said sternly. "We'll be dead if we don't try. And we've come too far to take this lying down."

"Agreed," Alayna said, standing beside him. "And I think it's time to discuss survivability moving forward. The hotel has been wonderful these last few days, but we need to find something more sustainable. If we're not careful, we'll run out of supplies, fast."

"I did use too many potatoes this morning," Norah whispered, cursing herself.

"Forget about it. We thought we'd be fried potatoes by now," Brandon assured Norah, patting her hand affectionately.

"Surely you were prepared for something like this," Clay said, looking toward Jacobs. "You were moving somewhere all too fast yesterday. Somewhere in your candy shop."

"That's right!" Daniels said, snapping his finger. "You were heading somewhere behind the store shelves. There was some kind of staircase—"

"That's the lab," Jacobs admitted, rolling his eyes. "The lab is beneath Moe's. And, yes, there are plenty of supplies down there. Water. Food. Even a bit of alcohol, although surely not enough for Ralph here." He skidded his foot across the ground, contemplating.

"Leland to the rescue," Clay said halfheartedly. "You have to let us down there. To gather supplies."

"I don't know. It's meant to be sealed from the public," Jacobs said, lifting his chin in hesitation.

"Are you kidding me? You can't use that excuse now," Alayna said. "The public might be a thing of the past. We're all we know. Even you, with all your knowledge about the nanites, haven't a clue if your family and friends are living or dead." Her eyes flashed with the seriousness of her words.

Jacobs moved toward the door, then, gesturing. "Fine. I'll let you in, if you're all in such a big rush."

64.

Deep beneath Moe's Candy, the research lab was a sterile, white-walled environment with massive vats of gooey liquid lining the sides. The survivors paraded lightly through it, eyeing the liquid with suspicion.

"That's the nanites," Jacobs affirmed. "We keep them in what we call jellyfish puree between rounds. Now, as we speak, those nanites are multiplying in the liquid, making it more and more saturated. Of course, they're harmless. The containers are airtight."

No one spoke, all skittish in front of the vats. They continued to amble toward the back of the lab, where another door led them down a long cement hallway and then into a kind of warehouse stocked with supplies. Mounds of bottled water, countless cans of beans and soup and vegetables, noodles, and—of course—candy, lined the walls and filled the center, towering over them.

"Shit," Brandon said, speaking for all of them. "You really are stocked."

The survivors began to scatter, perusing the many items and choosing what they thought they needed to head back to the hotel. In the back of Clay's mind, he wondered what purpose there was in returning to the hotel at all. This area was solid and airtight, hiding them from the outside world. But as he stood before the piles of crackers, Jacobs tapped him on the shoulder, gesturing toward a side room, an offshoot of the greater warehouse.

Without speaking, Clay followed him, wondering how much he should trust this man if his group was going to survive. Jacobs halted in front of another locked door and entered a code. The numbers buzzed and blued as he pressed them.

"What is this about?" Clay asked.

"Your symptoms," Jacobs said, eyeing him darkly. He shoved open the door and flipped on the light, revealing a skinny lab room. In a small drawer, he found a small tube filled with bead-like pills. He held it up to Clay. "You're going to need these," he said.

"What is it?" Clay asked, hesitant. He remembered that Jacobs had noticed his symptoms immediately, without declaring the cause. "What do I have?"

"I'm not quite sure what plagues you," Jacobs said, tilting his head. "But most of your signs point to radiation poisoning."

Clay's stomach dropped. He held the skinny tube in his hands, assessing the pills. "And these will cure me?"

"No," Jacobs affirmed. "Radiation poisoning has no cure. There's just treatment for symptoms. And you're lucky I have this. It's another item we've been developing. It has shown to be quite satisfactory in removing the radioactive contaminants from the body."

Clay nodded. He couldn't think concretely about this diagnosis. Not yet. It sounded too deadly, and too personal. He popped a pill into his mouth and swallowed it dry. “Okay. Let’s just keep this between us, then,” he said, gesturing to the others in the warehouse. “I have to be their leader.”

“I know the dynamic,” Jacobs affirmed. He patted Clay on the shoulder, attempting to generate some form of camaraderie. “Let’s join that rest, shall we? See what they’ve found.”

Clay and Jacobs walked back into the warehouse, discovering that their group stood in a small circle, without supplies, whispering. The moment they saw Clay, they broke apart, their faces grim. Alayna’s lips were tight.

“What is it?” he asked. “Why haven’t you gathered supplies?”

“We started to,” Alayna said slowly. “But then we realized that we might very well be some of the last people on earth. And it doesn’t make sense to sleep anywhere that isn’t locked tight, like this lab.”

Alayna’s words “the last people on earth” seemed to echo through the air.

Clay nodded slightly, trying to wrap his mind around their new world. They couldn’t be the only survivors, but until they knew otherwise, it was better to be safe than sorry. “Yeah, good thinking.” His shoulders slumped slightly. “Are there sleeping quarters down here, Leland?”

Jacobs nodded. “Several of our scientists stayed here, before the accident. Their rooms are down the hall. Safe. Tightly sealed. Appropriate for just this scenario.”

“And then,” Alayna said, “during the daytime tomorrow, we’ll start a hunt around town for more supplies. We can make a chart. See how much we need. Also, see how much freezer space we have. People stay alive in terrible circumstances all the time. And we've got the brains to make this work."

"Brilliant idea, Alayna," Norah said. "I've been canning things my entire life. I can help with the logistics. And the organization." She patted Brandon on the back, grinning. "We'll be proper hunter-gatherers. You hear that, Brandon?"

Brandon grinned at her and pumping his arm. "If you need anything at all, I'm your man."

Alayna grinned, turning her head toward Clay. He was conscious that they'd hardly touched each other all day, let alone spoken. He shivered. As they stood, their new plan stretching before them, they all heard a strange, terrible, unordinary sound.

The telephone had begun to ring.

65.

The phone rang a second time, echoing throughout the lab. The sound was ominous, coming from another, very distant world. Alayna's eyes were upon Clay, waiting for him to make a move.

"Who would be calling?" Clay finally spoke, turning to Jacobs.

Jacobs shrugged sharply, as nervous as the others. He took a step back, gesturing. "The cell towers were shut down days ago, but I didn't think of the landlines. It could be anyone from the outside."

They were all silent as the phone rang a fourth time. Clay shivered as he picked up the receiver. He swallowed and didn't speak, waiting for sound on the other end of the phone. It was like listening to a seashell.

Immediately, the phone began to blare in a robotic voice. "Greetings, valued customer. We would like to announce that you've won a trip to Cancun, all expenses paid. Congratulations! All you have to do—"

Clay dropped the phone back to its cradle. He didn't speak for a moment, until, suddenly, a slight smile stretched over his face. He turned to his fellow survivors.

"What was it?" Alayna whispered. They'd been unable to hear.

"A robocall. Telling me I'd won a vacation. How exciting," Clay smirked.

"Damn," Ralph said, his face crinkling. "It's the end of the world and we still can't escape those solicitors. Won't they leave us the hell alone?"

Brandon chuckled and Norah grinned. "You got that right," she agreed. "Won't leave me alone, even in this little hole in the ground. But I'll take that vacation, if they're offering."

Clay didn't respond, allowing her joke to hang in the air. He stood in quiet contemplation, gazing down at the phone, remembering what Jacobs had told them. The landlines were unchecked.

Ralph scratched at his growing white goatee and walked forward, lifting the phone. "Call my brother, maybe," he said, sniffing. "Over in North Carolina." He waited for the tone and then dialed. He paused, bringing all the survivors to stare at him, panicked, knowing they were about to learn so much.

But he shook his head, hanging up. "It's busy," he said. "That guy. He talks on the phone all the goddamn time. Probably just talking about the weather. Doesn't know what I'm up to. Haven't spoken in years."

Norah came, next. She dialed a number—her daughter's—and stood, waiting. But she shook her head, wordlessly.

"Busy?" Clay asked, already sensing the worst.

"Busy," Norah agreed.

They continued, much like this, dialing all the numbers they could remember. Everyone except Brandon. He seemed to slowly distance himself from the crowd, both emotionally and physically.

"Oh, come here, dear," Norah said as tears began to run down his face. She pulled him into a warm embrace, his sobs increasing in intensity as he lowered his head into her shoulder. "There's no one left for you, is there?"

Brandon shook his head, barely perceptible to the others. "If it makes you feel any better, hon, I'll be your family," Norah said, her eyes sad, and it was clear she was fighting back her own tears.

"Thanks," Brandon said as he righted himself, glancing around the room where all eyes were upon him. "I—I'll be all right. I'm sure I have a distant cousin twice removed out in the world somewhere."

"For what it's worth, champ, I think we're all a little bit family now," Ralph added, wiping a speck of dust from the corner of his eye. "I know we've only just found each other very recently, but I think I can speak for the rest of us when I say that we're here for each other."

The rest of the group nodded and smiled warmly. After only a few silent moments, it was Clay's turn at the telephone.

Clay felt numb as he dialed Valerie's number, knowing he wouldn't hear her voice on the other end. Immediately, after the busy signal began, he slammed the phone, sensing Alayna's eyes upon him. He ignored them, quivering.

"Did all of you dial cell phones? Or did you dial landlines?" he asked then, trying to find reason in this madness.

"Cell phone, course," Ralph said.

"Cell phone," Norah agreed. "I don't know anyone with a landline any more. No one but me."

Alayna stepped forward. "Are you thinking all the cell phone towers are down, not just ours?"

"Not sure," Clay said, staring down at the phone's face. The black buttons were menacing, now, offering so much disappointment. "I wonder if I can check my voice mail."

He dialed into his cellular service provider, waiting for his outgoing message. After a pause that seemed to stretch on forever, his prerecorded voice began. He stopped the recording by punching in his password easily—his daughter's birth date—and then waited, hearing the robotic woman tell him that he had seven new voice mails.

"Seven," he mouthed to Alayna, gesturing to the phone.

"Oh my god," Alayna whispered, her shoulders tense.

Seven felt like too many. Seven felt desperate.

Clay shifted his weight against the lab's block wall, gazing out, his eyes becoming bleary.

66.

The first was from Valerie. Her voice wasn't as light and friendly as he was used to, but it was her, and that was enough to cause his breath to catch.

"Hey, baby," she said. "Wanted to tell you we made it out past the edge of town, but just barely. Strangely, traffic is at a standstill. We've not moved in nearly an hour and there's no sign of that changing. Several of that wretched colonel's military cars have been blazing along the side of the road. I tried to wave one of them down to see what was going on, but they nearly ran me over, not even slowing to avoid me. Maia and I are staying positive though. She's still feeling warm from the flu, but we're going to schedule manicures just as soon as we pull into Austin. I'll get them painted that deep red that you like. Anyway, just thought I'd keep you updated. Maia and I both love you to pieces and can't wait until we're together again."

The next message was a bit more urgent. Valerie's voice was high-pitched, nervous—the one she reserved for those nights when he was a bit tardy after a shift. She worried about him. Always, to her worry, Clay had said, "It's just Carterville. We've moved here because it's safe. You know that."

"Hey, Clay. It's me again," the message began. "I know you're busy. But if you could call me as soon as you can, I really need to talk to you. They lied to all of us. As soon as we got moving again, they wouldn't let us off the road. We tried to turn onto highway six, but they had roadblocks put up. Now we're about to head into Helen, and from what it looks like from here, there are more roadblocks ahead. I really need to hear from you, Clay. Please call either Maia or my cell. Love you lots."

Concern caused Clay's brow to furrow, and he could feel the questioning eyes beat upon him from the group surrounding him. He pressed on.

Valerie sounded terribly hurried on the third message.

"Clay, I'm officially freaking out here. They've taken Maia to the infirmary because of the flu. I told them that she'd be fine with me, but the army doctor was insistent that they could help her." He heard her take a shaky breath. "And that bastard Colonel Wallace seems to have gotten his way after all. Everyone from Carterville has been quarantined here in Helen. They're not letting anyone leave. God, Clay. I'm so scared. I know you'll come when you can, but please make it quick."

Clay felt an impending sense of dread as the fourth message began, and then the fifth, and the sixth, all explaining that things were getting worse—that she needed him there.

Around Clay, the other survivors craned their necks, trying to listen to the messages. But the words were only for Clay.

Finally, the last message began, with a great howling from his beloved wife. "OH GOD, CLAY," it began, turning into a screech of fear. "OH GOD. I DON'T KNOW WHERE YOU ARE. But hurry. I don't know what's going on, but the entire town's gone crazy. The colonel said that you knew all about this. Is that true? People are talking, and rumor has it it's the whole world. Oh god, Clay, and they still won't tell me what happened to Maia. God, Clay. I really need you." As she spoke, Clay could picture her beautiful, tired eyes. He could remember the first time they'd kissed as teenagers, how he'd inhaled the scent of her and tucked her close to him in the back of his car.

The message crept on, and Clay had the sense that she was staggering around, her eyes manic, her voice lost to hysteria. After what seemed like an eternity, Clay began to hear gunshots in the distance. His wife screamed a final time—a gut-wrenching scream that forced the blood to drain from Clay's face.

He couldn't speak. He tapped the phone, forcing the message to play once more. And then again. He tried to get a sense for her surroundings—for any sense of hope. During the third run-through, he made eye contact with Alayna and then hit the speaker function on the phone, blaring out Valerie's scream to the survivors.

The moment the scream halted and the message stopped, Ralph punched his fist into his open palm, wrinkles pinching between his eyebrows. A sense of doom settled over the room—another low after a slight high. Clay clutched the phone to his chest, hearing his wife scream over and over again. He couldn't bring himself to stop.

67.

After several minutes more, Alayna came forward, taking the phone from Clay, and dropped it to the counter. She grabbed onto Clay's shoulders and shook him, attempting to bring him back to reality. "Clay!" she cried. "Clay. There's nothing you can do from here. Come on."

From here, Clay played over and over in his mind. Around them, the other survivors had grown hysteric. Brandon leaned heavily upon his knees, quivering. "It's all over. It's all really over," he said to himself.

Norah pushed her cane forward, her eyes to the ground. Ralph began to speak to himself, muttering Connie's name and some other unrecognizable gibberish. "So, it's true," he finally said for all to hear. "They're all dead now. And—"

"Maybe not," Clay spouted, stepping back. "Maybe they're not dead. We can't know that."

"We heard gunfire," Brandon said, scoffing. "What else do you think happened? You have to see the reality here, Clay. You're law enforcement. You know the world."

But Clay shook his head vehemently. "That gunfire doesn't mean that Valerie's dead," he said, beginning to pace. "Sure, the military had guns for the infected. Not for the innocent."

"Who's to say that your wife wasn't infected?" Ralph asked, his eyes far away.

"She didn't sound infected," Clay argued. "She wouldn't have called me if she was. That's not how this works." He said it with certainty, internally knowing that the more time passed, the less he seemed to know. He turned his eyes toward Jacobs, but the scientist had backed toward the corner, almost hiding from the rest of them.

"They were surely just killing the crazed," Clay declared with finality. "No one else."

Daniels burst forward then, chiming in. "Well then, does that mean you think that people are generally alive outside of our quasi-safe zone? Outside of this contained energy field? Even with all those crazed monsters out there, infecting each other, tearing into one another?" His eyes were fierce, bright. He was shifting into action mode, as he'd been trained. And Clay's inability to "see the truth," in Daniels's eyes, wouldn't get in the way.

Clay breathed heavily. His mind raced, turning the images of his wife and daughter over and over in his mind. They had to be safe. They had to be okay. He remembered teaching Maia to shoot a gun just the year before, how she'd blasted through the center of the target. He'd told her she was a deadeye. She'd rolled her own eyes, scoffing slightly, but accepted the compliment. "Whatever, Dad. Not like I'll ever need it."

God, how wrong they'd been. Wrong about everything. Wrong about the very way in which he spent his life, spent his time. He felt Alayna's fingers at the nape of his neck, kneading at his skin—a reminder that she was still there for him, body and soul. But this assurance felt dead.

Jacobs stepped toward the phone, finally making an effort. Clay looked at him as if he were alien. He lifted the phone and addressed the survivors. "It doesn't do us any good to panic," he said.

"What do you care?" Brandon asked then. "You were perfectly fine allowing us to die before. You didn't even tell us about the location of the bomb until it was almost too late. It's like you want the world to end."

"And you started all of this!" Ralph sneered from the corner. His face was pale, gaunt. He looked older and more ragged with each passing moment.

Jacobs gave them a simple smile. "If you want to point your finger at me, that's perfectly fine. I know every someone needs someone else to detest. And I've become that persona."

Alayna sneered. Clay turned toward her, lifting a finger. "Let's listen to what he has to say," he said.

Jacobs continued seamlessly. "I think we should call another lab. A friend of mine works in Minneapolis, and I heard from him as recently as four days ago. He was perfectly fine. Microwaving a frozen dinner, in fact, and minding his own business. No sign of crisis."

A small spark of hope lit in Clay's heart. Jacobs dialed the number then pressed the speakerphone button, his eyes grey and blank. The phone blared out a ringing sound as it connected to the tucked-away lab in Minnesota, but no one answered. Thirty seconds of wait turned to two minutes, and still the survivors' eyes remained upon Jacobs.

Finally, he hung up and then dialed another lab. And then another. As he dialed each one, his shoulders slumped forward more and more, making him look like a crooked question mark. He was defeated.

As the tension stretched between them, Clay clapped his hands together, getting their attention once more. “Listen, everyone,” he said, his mind teetering on insanity. As he spoke, he structured some semblance of a plan, recognizing that his troops needed something to keep morale up. As it was, he saw suicide plots in each of their eyes.

“The voice mails from my wife were more than twenty-four hours old, which means there’s no possible way to know what’s going on.” His voice was firm and confident. “Which means we have to make moves without knowing. I say we should move on to Helen—maybe get all the way to Earlton, where the military base is.”

“All the way to Earlton?” Brandon asked, raising his eyebrows. “We can’t even get out of Carterville. You saw what happened to Connie.”

It seemed that after constant devastation, people had allowed themselves to forget about Connie. But people ticked their eyes toward Ralph now, who looked stumped with sorrow.

“That’s right,” Daniels spouted then. “The energy field is controlled from the outside.”

“And there’s absolutely nothing we can do?” Alayna asked.

Daniels shook his head, unable to look at her. “Unfortunately, no. We’re relegated to our fate within the containment zone.” His voice was matter-of-fact, even as it delivered such devastating news. “I’m sorry.”

Norah began to shake, then. She cowered to the ground, peppering the concrete with her tears. “It was fine to die,” she murmured. “It was fine to die alone. But the entire world is falling now. It’s the end times. The devil. He walks among us."

The survivors stood without speaking, the dial tone wailing from the phone that remained off the hook. Clay closed his eyes, feeling a howl of despair try to clamber from his chest. But he kept his lips tightly sealed.

68.

That night, the survivors slept fitfully in their barracks in the basement lab. Clay found himself lying alone, despite Alayna's pleas of wanting to be with him after such a tragic afternoon. But now that he'd survived the day, Clay couldn't stop beating himself up about being unfaithful to Valerie. Would she understand and forgive him if she truly knew the reasoning behind the infidelity? He hoped that he would be able to find out.

Clay entered the lab kitchen early in the morning to find both Daniels and Brandon standing, steaming coffee mugs in hand. They didn't speak for a few moments as Clay poured himself a cup. He wondered what people had said on the Titanic, right before it had dipped into the ocean. He supposed nothing would have sounded appropriate.

"There's been some power fluctuations," Daniels said then. "The town's been flickering on and off all night and this morning."

"I see," Clay said. "Any consequences to the lab?"

Daniels shook his head. "The lab seems to be battery powered. It should last for years, if we want it to."

"Great. So we can just lie around here while the rest of the world burns," Brandon said.

"Don't," Clay said, slicing his hand through the

air. "We don't need your pissy attitude right now. Think about Norah. She's on the edge and you're not helping."

Brandon bowed his head. The cut had been deep, given Brandon and Norah's budding friendship.

"Did you go outside this morning, then?" Clay asked Daniels. "Anything else suspicious? Any sign of the crazed?"

"Only a few stragglers," Daniels said, smacking at his gun holster. "Their brains are all over the pavement now. Disgusting creatures."

Clay's thought—that these creatures used to be their neighbors and friends—had no meaning for him any longer. He sighed wearily before resting his coffee mug on the counter and heading toward the exit. He bounded up the steps toward the store entrance. Outside, he stared at the desolate waste of his once-beloved town. The corner stop sign was spattered with dried monster blood. Clay didn't peer around the corner, certain he'd discover the ruined bodies.

As he stood, he watched as the stoplight began to flicker before turning black for a full minute. He imagined the next several years of their life in the barracks—that is, if the supplies lasted that long—all the while not knowing what had occurred on the outside. For all they knew, the world outside was humming along fine.

He had to get out. He had to discover the truth.

He marched back into the lab, discovering Daniels in thinker mode, his chin rested on his fist. The sterile lights from the lab made his black stubble look all the more stark.

"When the power goes out, wouldn't that make the energy field flicker as well?" Clay asked.

Daniels's eyes slid toward him. "I assume so," he

said. "Absolutely."

"If we could figure out the pattern of the fluctuations, we could free ourselves," Clay said. "Just walk directly out of the containment zone without bursting all over the pavement." His words were harsh. He was grateful the others were still tucked in their beds.

Daniels stood. He shook his head vehemently. "I think that's a foolish idea," he declared. "The energy field has been set up for a reason."

"But those reasons don't exist any longer," Clay said.

"But imagine what would happen if it flickered for just a moment. In the flash of an eye, the green orb would come down over you, and you'd be dust. Just like Connie. And then what would these people do?"

Clay tilted his head. "I thought you were of the 'kill or be killed' mentality?"

"Sure. For me," Daniels continued. "But you're a man of the people. You're supposed to stay. To keep them safe. They look to you, Clay. You're the Carterville Sheriff, for god's sake."

"But there isn't a Carterville anymore," Clay said, smashing his fist against the countertop. "And if we don't move now and get some kind of help, maybe we won't die today. Or tomorrow. And we might still be scrapping away like rats in a few years. But that's no kind of life, Adam."

Daniels shrugged. "It's your lot in life, now, Clay. The moment you were elected—"

"The moment I was elected, I didn't know I'd lose my wife and daughter. And they were all I had in the world," Clay hissed.

As he spoke, he sensed a presence behind him.

Daniels's eyes turned upward, gazing at the doorway. Clay turned to find the entire troop of survivors glaring at him, their arms crossed and plastered against their chests. Their anger and fear were palpable.

* * * *

Far from the laboratory basement, near Crawford Farm, the translucent energy field flashed off, making Carterville just more flat land on which to roam.

A few feet away, a large swarm of the crazed monsters, blood dripping down their cheeks to their chests, bucked forward and into the town containment zone. The world was theirs for the taking. And they were hungry.

Moments later, the energy field flickered to life once again, sealing in Carterville's latest guests.

69.

Alarmed, Alayna raised her hand, her voice cutting through the tense air of the lab kitchen. "Clay. Daniels is right. You can't go out there and just try to 'get lucky' with the energy barrier. We have no way to know when the power outages come and go. They're brand new for us. We need to assess them first—for days or weeks maybe—before making any such decision."

Clay understood, then, as he gazed into Alayna's eyes, that she wasn't with him. Perhaps she couldn't be any longer. The world they'd cultivated had imploded. And now every person was alone. There were no more companions. There were no more truces.

"I have to do this," Clay said. "I have to get out there. I need to find them."

He offered no other explanation.

He began to pack a large backpack, filling it with enough supplies for at least a week of being on the other side. As he packed, he felt strangely centered. He could no longer feel the angry stares from the other survivors, who almost assuredly knew that they would soon have to fend for themselves, without him. Norah, the weakest of the group, sat in the corner as he packed, praying for him. Her words weren't a comfort.

Clay's backpack, stocked with water bottles and matches and granola bars and nuts, felt strangely light on his back as he lifted it. He nodded toward his fellow survivors with finality, and then he turned toward the exit door, already anxious to feel the ground beneath his feet.

But the survivors followed him, scampering after him like abandoned animals. He could feel Daniels hot on his heels.

"Adam, nothing you say can change my mind," Clay said. "This is the only way I can see to find resolution. I can't live like this, not knowing what has become of them."

Daniels didn't respond. Neither did the others. They followed Clay up the steps, Norah's knees creaking as she walked. A gumball was squashed beneath Clay's boot, and the fresh air tasted good on his tongue. He needed these last sensations before the grimness of the outside world was revealed to him.

On Main Street, he turned back to find his group of survivors in a single line near the storefront, their eyes upon their feet. They looked skittish. Alayna wrapped her arm around Norah's shoulder, whispering to her. Clay felt his stomach drop.

But during this moment of brief nostalgia, he heard something. He turned his head toward the street corner, noting the shadow that began to form across the pavement. And before he could say anything, an entire horde of the crazed came rushing toward them, their arms flailing and their lesions bleeding languidly.

Norah shrieked. One of the crazed slouched toward her, his teeth barely missing her shoulder blade before Brandon shoved him, full force, to the pavement. Daniels blasted a bullet through the monster's brain, and the splattering blood painted the approaching horde. One of the crazed licked his lips, as if he liked the taste of his friend.

As if on autopilot, Clay burst forward and ripped his gun from his holster, aiming at the mutants' brains and pummeling them to the ground. "GET NORAH INSIDE!" he cried to Brandon before blasting the crazed flailing toward the teenager and the old woman. "HIDE. GET OUT OF THE WAY." He continued to blast, one after another, his eyes filling with panic and rage. "COME ON."

Daniels, Alayna, and Clay rampaged, then, destroying one crazed monster after another, lining their boots with the blood of the dead. Ralph was in the center of them, flailing a large stick he'd picked up from the ground, bucking their bodies sideways. Clay focused upon the miscreation beside Ralph, blasting it seconds before it attacked. But he knew they were losing time, and it seemed that the crazed kept rushing from beyond the corner.

"RALPH. GET DOWNSTAIRS!" he cried, blasting two more crazed, then grasping Ralph's collar and flinging him toward the door of the candy shop. He felt menacing, like an animal or a warrior. But they were running out of ammunition, and it seemed they would be eaten at any moment.

Daniels reached toward his back, then, and revealed a menacing automatic weapon. He screamed, "CLAY! ALAYNA! GET BACK!" And then he began to spit bullets at the mutants. Each line fell back upon the ground, slamming against the pavement. And then, when another line came roaming toward them, he blasted them to the ground as well. Clay watched the carnage, trying not to recognize any of the monsters' faces or think about their names. He was breathless, his eyes bulging as the minutes continued and the bodies built a mountain in front of the candy store. The rest of the survivors were huddled at the entrance, watching, Brandon's arms wrapped around Norah to hold her standing.

Finally, after what seemed like forever, Daniels stood huffing, tilting his gun skyward, without another crazed to destroy. His eyes were manic and almost yellow, and he breathed heavily, spitting.

"Jesus," Alayna gasped. "Where the hell did they all come from?"

Jacobs stepped out of the storefront. "My guess is with all these power fluctuations we've been experiencing, the perimeter energy field is also wavering."

Clay turned to the other survivors, who eyed him with fear and confusion. He gestured toward the bodies, knowing he looked crazed. "You see? Just as I thought," he told them. "We are no safer here, in the center of Carterville, than we would be on the road. I think we can make it through the energy field during a down phase, which seems to be happening more and more often."

"But we'll be killed on the road, too," Ralph spat. "And military man here doesn't have an endless supply of bullets." His ears dripped with blood. A scratch had formed down his cheek, from the monsters, but he appeared unbitten.

"We just need to make it to Earlton," Clay said. "That's all."

"But we tried to call them," Norah reminded him.

"As far as we know, just the physical phone lines are down. We'll only know for sure if we can make it to the military base. And we also know that the military base is safe and stocked with supplies, if things get too bad out there." Clay swallowed.

Ralph muttered something to Brandon that Clay couldn't hear. And Brandon nodded succinctly, squeezing Norah's upper arm. Behind her stood Jacobs, always in the background, leering. Clay's adrenaline was so high he wanted to punch him in the face for all the devastation that he'd caused.

"We don't really see another way, now," Brandon finally said. "We'll come with you. And we'll die with you, if that's what it comes to."

Ralph nodded, and Norah's eyes burned with a sudden passion. "We'll not go down without a fight," she said.

70.

Clay and the survivors gathered back in the basement to reassess their plans. Clay felt Alayna's hand at the small of his back as he stood at the coffeemaker. She shook slightly, and Clay turned to her, placing his hands on her shoulders.

"You doing okay?" he asked her, tilting his head. "Really, I mean."

"I'm fine," she murmured, her eyes far away. She bit her lip, her words coming soft and intimate. "I'm just . . . better knowing you're not going alone, is all."

Clay nodded. He felt the same but remained silent about it.

"And I'm so sorry about your wife and Maia," Alayna whispered. "I know you must be feeling a strange range of emotions right now. And I know I must be far from your mind, in so many respects. But know that I'm here for you."

Before Clay could respond, Brandon and Norah entered the kitchen from the side, both holding on to backpacks filled with various supplies, including fruit and bottles of water. Brandon zipped his heartily, explaining that the others were packing up and would be ready to leave within the hour.

"How do you think we should go out that way, anyway?" Brandon asked, his eyebrow high. "There's seven of us now, which is too many to go in a single vehicle."

Clay tilted his head, realizing he hadn't thought this through. "Shit. You're right," he said. "Not even Adam can take all of us."

"Could we go in separate cars?" Alayna asked. "A few of us in your cruiser, and then the rest of us with Daniels? We were doing that before. It seemed to work all right."

A feeling of dread passed over Clay. He imagined being helpless in his vehicle while another, containing his newfound family, burst into flames before being overtaken by the crazed. There would be nothing he could do.

"I don't want to split up," he declared.

Jacobs, Ralph, and Daniels entered from the warehouse, their lips thin. Daniels looked like he'd just returned from war. "What is it?" he asked, sensing that the conversation had turned.

"I think we need to locate a vehicle that can haul all of us, including our supplies," Clay said. "Do you know anyone with a big van that might have been left behind?"

"I don't know anyone in this town," Jacobs said. "This is your territory."

In the silence that followed, no one stepped forward with knowledge. Norah said something about her old pickup truck but remembered that she'd given it to her daughter nearly ten years before. Brandon shrugged sharply. The future seemed bleak.

Then Daniels turned toward Ralph, assessing him. "You look like you're in deep thought. Anyone you know keeping something around? Something big?"

Ralph kicked his heels as he walked, pouring himself a cup of coffee. It was clear that he sensed he had an audience, and he held their attention. "Well, well. Let's see. Old Mike, he was working on something at that mechanic station across town. That old one off Jefferson Avenue. He told me about it. An old Humvee, actually."

"That would be perfect," Clay said, suddenly thrilled. "You know for a fact it's there?"

"That's what he said. Don't think he would have taken it out of town. The old bastard, Mike, I'm certain he didn't leave his place, even. Probably one of those monsters now."

Everyone was silent for a while, allowing Ralph's words to register.

"You should know, though, I don't know what its condition is. Mike was an asshole and a drunk, and I'd say that he wasn't all there in the head, especially in the past few months. So the car might work. Or it might not." Ralph shrugged.

"Well it sounds like the best chance we have," Clay said.

In the silence that followed, they heard a clattering in the store above: an alert that more of the crazed were coming.

Daniels gripped his automatic weapon and set his jaw. "I'll go get more bullets from my bag," he said, then disappeared through the side door.

"We can't rely on Adam for every attack. I think if we're all going to be out on the streets, we should be armed," Alayna said, glancing from person to person, resting her gaze upon Jacobs a few seconds longer than the rest. "Every one of us."

71.

After gathering their things, the survivors stood at the other side of the candy shop's hidden door, Daniels at the front holding his gun like a beacon. He bowed his head and then kicked the door in, revealing a barrage of the crazed scrambling over the gumballs and chocolate bars, their eyes dripping.

Daniels blasted through them. The survivors watched as bodies crumbled to the floor, while stray bullets burst through the candy shop window, forcing stray glass shards to flash through the air aimlessly. Daniels gestured forth, and the seven of them loaded into multiple cars before heading toward their first destination.

Clay opened the back warehouse of the sheriff's station, where they kept the guns in reserve, realizing that this utilization of keys in locks was now an antiquated thing—that the world was now a dangerous, unlocked place. He flung the key to the warehouse floor and began passing handheld guns to Ralph, Norah, and Brandon, before handing a final one to Jacobs, who held it like a toy. Clay couldn't help but judge him: this science boy who'd decided that the world was his playground. And now he could hardly protect himself in the face of its uproar.

After retrieving the guns, they began their trek across the empty town, eyeing the familiar once-warm coffee shops, the gas stations, and the houses without trust. Despite their previous attempt to sweep the town, any one of them could contain more of the crazed. Any one of them could contain their death.

"It's strange. I remember I met Megan at that bar once," Alayna whispered, pointing. "She was the most beautiful human I'd ever seen. I was so confused, then. About life, my career, my sexuality . . ." her thoughts drifted off. "And now look at it."

The bar's front window was blasted open, the bar stools crooked.

The mechanic shop was two miles away. The survivors drove in silence: Clay, Alayna, Norah, and Ralph in the lead vehicle, and Daniels, Brandon, and Jacobs bringing up the rear. Clay turned his head from side to side as Ralph pointed out the tucked-away mechanic shop. "Ayup," Ralph said. "There it is. I see it through that dirty window."

Clay stopped his cruiser and Daniels pulled up beside him. As they neared the entrance, he saw that Ralph's observation was correct. The military-like Humvee sat just inside. It was open, its insides gleaming from the daylight that filtered in through the window. It had recently been worked on, but the mechanic—Ralph's old pal—had long since fled.

The storage unit's lock was rusted and easily broken with a firm kick from Daniels's military boot. They opened the door, watching as it slid up, revealing the huge vehicle.

"It's practically a tank," Brandon said, impressed. "And it can store all of our supplies." He walked around the back, noting the size of its rear.

"Why would a Carterville man buy something like this?"

"Mike was mad," Ralph said. He rubbed his fingers together, eyeing the insides of the Humvee. "He wasn't finished. You can see here—he was in the middle of restructuring these pipes."

"Is it something we can fix ourselves?" Clay asked, knowing his level of mechanical ability was novice.

"Sure. I can start right now," Ralph said, eyeing the tools near the corner. "Left everything out, the fool. But we're going to need some oil and some gas, and of course"—he tapped the innards of the vehicle—"I think we're going to need to charge up the battery. But we can get a jump from one of our vehicles. Connie always said it was foolish how much I studied up on our cars. Always getting grease all over the living room. But now, she'd be proud." He looked up, his eyes misty. Clay had an abstract memory of the couple arguing together, bickering, showing not a single shred of love.

"Perfect," Clay said, slapping Ralph on the shoulder. "Let's get cracking, then. Tell us what to do. You're the boss now."

"We're at your service," Brandon agreed, no longer the small, maniacal teenager he'd been just days before. He was quickly becoming a man.

And for a moment, as Clay watched his team join together for survival, he felt a strange sense of pride.

72.

Despite their effort, the repairs proved to be slow and monotonous. Ralph began to bark out orders, unable to understand why Brandon couldn't do simple mechanical repairs correctly, and occasionally asking him if he'd even been born a man.

Clay kept watch outside of the garage as Alayna and Daniels headed out to look for gas. They returned with several cans of it, the gas sloshing around in the containers, looking pleased.

Every few hours, a scattering of the crazed would meander toward them, allowing several chances for them to practice blasting them in the brains. Alayna tried to show Norah how to hold her gun, but Norah balked, telling Alayna, "I've been around a long, long time," before piercing a crazed directly between the eyebrows.

Alayna gazed at her, impressed. "I don't think I've ever loved anyone more than I love you right now," she laughed.

Norah looked at her work, shivering slightly. Clay approached her, remembering how he'd felt when he'd first killed one of the crazed—Cliff, what felt so long ago in that jail cell. "It gets easier," he said. "Both physically and mentally. It gets easier. I promise."

Norah nodded, understanding. It was unspoken that what they were going through was horrendous but absolutely necessary. They were building a life for themselves, and that meant they had to stop feeling nostalgic for all time that had passed. Even Clay had been able to fight back emotions about his wife and daughter, turning a clear eye to the issue at hand.

As Clay stood keeping watch, Jacobs approached him, stuffing his hands into his pockets. They spoke quietly, not wanting the others to hear.

"How are you feeling since taking the medicine? For the radiation?" Jacobs asked.

"Actually, I'm feeling good, all things considered," Clay affirmed, realizing he'd actually forgotten about many of his symptoms since taking that first pill. "My hair seems to be staying in now, thank god. And I haven't felt a single bout of nausea."

"Good," Jacobs said, nodding his head succinctly. "It's strange, this radiation. Especially given that the meteorite issue was fabricated."

"Sure. But the meteorite actually did fall," Clay said, his eyebrows high. "I saw it in the ground, steaming. It was about as real as they come."

"Well then you were probably affected," Jacobs said. "With that close range, you probably picked up a small bit of the radiation, or something similarly poisonous. Without assessing the actual meteorite myself, I can't know for sure. I'm incredibly curious, but I didn't bring the right equipment to go check it out myself."

Clay held up his hand. "I wouldn't worry about it. What happened happened. And I'm not dead yet, right?" He flashed an ironic smile, listening to the clank of his mechanics in the garage.

"There's just no way to know what we're dealing with, here," Jacobs affirmed, his eyes dark. "With radiation, you don't know how it will rear its ugly head. So be alert. I have to admit, now, all of these people are counting on you to pull them through, at least until we get to Earlton." He spoke with pessimism, watching as Norah blasted another crazed through its soft skull. "I just don't want you to get your hopes up about your personal survival."

Clay allowed the words to sink in. Strangely, they didn't seem to affect him or bring him panic. His entire existence remained in finding his family. Assuring these people remained okay was secondary. Third was his own life. He'd live as long as he could in the interim. No matter what.

73.

Although the repairs were taking longer than he'd like, time seemed to tick along too quickly. Night would fall soon. Clay shifted his weight, clinging to his gun, with the echo of the bullet he'd just shot throttling through his ears. The two crazed, both women wearing black dresses, were splattered across the pavement. They all needed to get going, and soon.

Clay turned to the group. Ralph and Brandon were cranking at the interior of the vehicle, and Norah was organizing the supplies they'd been able to bring with them from the lab. He cleared his throat and addressed them all, his hands upon his hips. He felt Alayna's dark eyes upon him. Always, she was watching.

"Hear me out, everyone," he said.

The survivors turned, expectant. They'd heard him out so many times. With grease on their faces, they waited.

"I think we should split into two groups," Clay began.

"You already said that's too dangerous," Ralph interrupted, sweeping his hand over the vehicle. "That's why we're doing this, Clay. Jesus."

Clay shook his head, feeling more and more certain of his opinion. "Just listen. In the end, we'll be safer with this one vehicle. But seeing as it's taking a while, we could be more useful if we split up. We've been here for hours, and it's almost nightfall. We should gather more supplies before we get going."

"But what about what we already have back at the hotel and the lab?" Jacobs asked.

"We can't be sure it'll be enough. Besides, we need more nonperishable goods and possibly some medical supplies."

"You want two groups, one for supplies and one to finish off the vehicle?" Alayna asked. She offered a soft layer of support, giving him a brief smile.

"I don't think that's a terrible idea, I suppose," Daniels offered. He scratched at his growing beard. "I'll stay here with the mechanics if you want to head off and find supplies, Clay. I think you should move quickly, though."

Clay began dividing the group, feeling like a postapocalyptic dodgeball captain. "Ralph, you and Brandon and Daniels stay here. Norah, take a rest here, if you like. We need you in tip-top shape for when we get moving. Daniels, make sure Norah's sleeping in a place you can see her. We can't afford to lose anyone else."

Daniels shot his hand to his forehead, saluting. "These power outages are becoming more and more prevalent. Maybe . . ." Daniels began, drifting his sight up to the fading sunset, when Clay continued.

"And that means Jacobs, Alayna, and I will go gather up as many supplies as we can in this immediate area. We'll go on foot and leave the cars here to use for a light source while you finish with the repairs," Clay continued. He shuffled toward the edge of the driveway, watching as Alayna and Jacobs stepped forward, joining him. "I've never trusted us more as a team than I do right now," he affirmed.

"Keep it up, everyone, and we just might live through this. We just damn well might."

74.

Behind the garage, a backcountry road cut down about a half mile, past a forest of densely packed trees, before opening out on a street of farmhouses. Clay and Alayna walked side by side, Jacobs following up behind them, as they headed toward the first of the residences. No one bothered to speak.

The first farmhouse, which belonged to a widow named Teresa, was almost empty. Just a few suitcases had been placed in the first room, half stocked, before Teresa's ultimate flee from Carterville. Clay wandered through the house, feeling like an intruder, gazing at the photographs of Teresa's deceased husband that lined the fireplace and walls.

Alayna appeared beside him, holding a bag of painkillers and other medications and giving him a knowing look. "Seems like we'll need these eventually, huh?"

"Good find," Clay agreed, skimming his fingers over the top of the counter. "Did Leland find anything?"

"He's in the garage, actually," Alayna said, shivering. "But the woman was so alone up here. She didn't keep a lot. Not even food. I remember I saw her at the diner frequently. She didn't often cook."

"Right," Clay said, heading toward the exit. "Then

we shouldn't waste our time diving through her ghosts."

They went to the next farmhouse, and then the next, finding nothing but a few food items and another tank of gas. The last house on the left was a one-story that used to belong to a model citizen of the town—a man named Rex Taylor—who'd often come by Clay's house to play cards and drink beers on the back porch. Despite having known the man for several years, Clay realized he'd never been inside Rex's home. He reached for the door, and then, finding it locked, barreled his boot into the door, waiting for it to give.

But the door didn't budge. Clay tilted his head, trying to see in through the door window, but found that it was blocked out, like a board was nailed across it, keeping intruders out.

"Whose house is this?" Alayna asked, appearing beside him. "Leland tried to get in from the back, but no dice."

"It's my friend Rex's," Clay admitted. "He wasn't a private guy, really. I expected him to be the type to just keep the door wide open, you know?"

"Ha. Well, when you leave your house for who knows how long, you probably at least lock it," Alayna said. "Did you try kicking it?"

"Of course," Clay said, incredulous. "I'm thinking about shooting it."

Alayna marched toward the side window and then noted that the glass, which was initially covered with lace curtains on the other side, was actually decoration for a dark stone that seemed to cover the entire interior of the house. Clay's jaw dropped, realizing that what she said was true. "I swear, I've seen him enter the house from his front door," Clay offered, shaking his head. "Or have I?"

"HEY!" Jacobs called to them from the back of the house, causing them both to scamper around the bushes and trees to find him staring at something on the ground.

Clay, thinking it was one of the crazed or perhaps another kind of danger, brought his gun from his holster and barreled toward Jacobs, adrenaline pumping through him. "What is it?" he cried.

Jacobs just pointed downward, waiting. Clay reached his side. There before them was a small door that seemed to go directly into the ground, its handle sticking straight into the air.

"What the hell?" Alayna asked, gasping for oxygen after the mad dash. "I don't understand."

Jacobs reached down and grasped the handle, yanking at it. To his surprise, the door crept open, causing him to cry out. "Grab on to it! My god, it's heavy!"

Clay gripped the edge of the cement door to help him lift but nearly ripped it from its hinges instead. Jacobs tumbled back as Clay flipped the bulky hatch over onto the barren ground, revealing a dark, dirt tunnel that seemed to ultimately turn into a staircase.

Alayna eyes went wide. "You said you knew this guy? Did you know that his house was essentially a fortress?"

Clay shook his head. He carefully lowered his legs into the tunnel and then dropped, catching himself on the side wall so he wouldn't tumble down the steps. Pain swept up and down his legs upon landing, but he soon righted himself, shouting up to Alayna and Jacobs. "Don't come down! I'll just check it out real quick like. Keep watch for any of the crazed."

Clay crept down the steps, searching for some kind of light switch. He slipped the flashlight from his holster and peered into the darkness before marching into an underground circular room filled with weapons.

Every sort of assault rifle lined the walls. Clay counted to ten, and then lost track, realizing that they extended to the far end of the cavernous room. Across from the rifles was Rex's collection of grenades and grenade launchers, every make and model. Clay shifted his weight. "I'll be damned," he said, remembering how Rex had been a vegetarian and seemed to take offense at curse words. "Was it all an act?"

He collected several of the weapons, oddly giddy that he'd discovered the selection. But as he carried them through the tunnel, back toward Alayna and Jacobs, he realized he hadn't seen Rex at the town meeting. In fact, he hadn't seen Rex in weeks.

"Holy mother of god," Alayna said, collecting the guns in her arms as he crawled from the tunnel. "Did you know he was like this?"

Clay shook his head vehemently. "I had no idea, honestly. And I realized that I didn't see him leave, either. Do you think he's still around?"

Alayna considered this, a darkness passing over her face. "You know, actually, now that you mention it, I think I heard from someone in town that Rex was leaving for a few weeks. He was visiting a friend, or he had a job out of town. It might have been both." She shrugged, but still eyed Clay suspiciously. "Why?"

"Just curious," Clay said, walking back between the trees and toward the mechanic shop. "We should get back with the others now. The sun's too low. It's making me nervous. And I don't like it."

75.

Clay trudged down the street with Alayna and Jacobs rushing behind him, chasing the shadows to get back to the Humvee before full-on darkness. The guns and other equipment clattered in their arms. They hadn't spoken in several minutes, the realization sharp between them that words wouldn't do any longer.

Once they were back at the mechanic shop, Ralph made a final crank in the Humvee before wiping his oil-laden hands over his pants and giving Brandon a slight nudge. "See, boy? Using your hands isn't so bad, after all."

Brandon agreed, giving both Norah and Ralph a wide smile. They slammed the hood shut and began positioning guns in the back of the Humvee.

They turned to Clay with trustful eyes, knowing that no matter how fatigued he was, his brain was constantly pushing forward, attempting to keep them alive.

"I think we should pack up as many supplies as we can and then get some rest back at the lab," he said. "We're exhausted. And it'll do no good for us to head out to the perimeter when we can barely walk. We're going to need our wits about us."

Norah cleared her throat, alerting them to her clear inability to be physical. Clay turned a sharp eye to her, explaining, "Norah, you know we'll carry you across that energy field if we have to. We're not leaving you behind."

"I just don't want to hold anyone back," she answered, looking at him sharply. "If I have to stay behind, I will."

"We're not leaving you," Brandon interrupted forcefully. "You know we wouldn't do that to you. We aren't just individuals trying to survive. We're a team."

Norah nodded at him gratefully.

"I think that sounds fine," Ralph finally answered. "The Humvee's up and running, and we can take it back with us to the lab. Rest up. Get a move on."

Daniels got into the driver's seat and eased the Humvee from the garage bay. As they began to pile in, three of the crazed scrambled around the corner, blood oozing from between their teeth. Norah shot one in the brain, plastering it against the sidewalk, while Ralph killed the other two. Clay looked on with a burst of pride before helping them both into the Humvee. They rode silently back into town, toward the lab, eyeing the muted town around them.

Daniels tried to get as close to the candy shop as possible, but the presence of numerous abandoned cars forced him to park on a side street, a half block away from the entrance.

The team paraded into the blaring light of the laboratory, grateful to be out of the openness, where the crazed saw them as their next meal. They ate their own meal of potatoes, noodles, vegetables, and alcohol brought over from the hotel, chewing and glugging without words. For many nights, since this had all begun, they'd known that the following day didn't hold any certainty. And now that they were leaving the safety of the containment zone, everything was even more up in the air. They hadn't seen the outside world. They didn't know if they would find an entire world of destruction or if they would learn that they could live normally out there, as if nothing had happened.

Clay chose not to think about the possibilities and to just proceed, with his survival instincts in tow and without any sense of hope.

They went to bed immediately after eating. Clay and Alayna shared a room but not a bed. Clay lay awake listening to the quiet of Alayna's breathing, his eyes staring into the darkness of their barrack.

Sometime at around five in the morning—not that time had any meaning in this current reality—the light from the main room of the laboratory cut out. The violence of total darkness made Clay's eyes snap open. He was immediately awake, and he ripped from his bed and into the lab, stubbing his toes against a large box of supplies that they'd gathered for their departure.

"SHIT!" he cried.

A few other survivors began to clamber from their beds to join him. Jacobs gasped, incredulous. "But the backup battery system. I didn't think—"

"You didn't think it could go out?" Clay asked, almost disdainfully. "You didn't think the world would end with the nanites, either."

No one spoke at this. Jacobs snapped his fingers, remembering. "I think we have another backup system. It should kick on when the first one fails." As the team waited, an eerie light glowed across them, emanating from the ceiling's emergency fixtures. This cast long, strange shadows across the floor and turned their faces green. Alayna and Clay made momentary eye contact, feeling the strangeness of this new environment.

"All right," Clay said. "I think we should pack up the Humvee with our last-minute supplies now. No use in waiting here in this half light. And the sun's about to rise."

Everyone agreed. Norah grabbed a bag of fruits and vegetables—things, she said, they would ultimately missed if they couldn't get them on the outside. "We'll have to eat them quickly. And really appreciate them. Maybe write down the feeling of eating an apple for our future selves to remember it best."

Brandon wrapped his arms around the old woman, holding her tight. "Thank god you're here," he said. "Otherwise, we wouldn't look at the world correctly. We'd see only darkness."

As they neared the laboratory door, Clay felt a shadow descend over his heart. The dangers on the main roads were apparent, especially given that they'd killed countless of the crazed the previous day. He was certain they were still coming, especially with the power fully out now. And he had no idea if they could communicate with each other and thus tell other of the crazed their location.

"Daniels and I will lead," Clay announced, moments before he opened the door to the staircase that would take them into the candy shop. "And Alayna, you'll bring up the rear. You all have your guns still. Be prepared to fight if you have to. And we'll get the fuck out of here in no time."

No one spoke. Clay lifted the latch of the lab door, revealing the ghostly, grey light of the early morning. He took steps upward, feeling the others close behind him. He could hear subtle noises from Norah's creaking bones. But she didn't complain.

When they reached the sales floor of the candy store, the exterior of the shop looked empty and abandoned, just as quiet as it had been the previous evening. Clay raised his hands, speaking quietly. "Okay. The Humvee is just around the corner. Let's be cautious and alert. But it looks like this might be our best chance. No matter what, this is our first step to life on the outside. After this, there's no going back."

The team nodded, their eyes dark and serious. And then Clay took the first steps to daylight, feeling the weight of six other peoples' lives upon his shoulders. He didn't know how to pray for them.

76.

The lone survivors of Carterville stood at the entrance of Moe's, blinking into the early sunlight. Clay placed his hand upon his holster, looking around. He sensed something. Suddenly, they heard the slobbering and growling noise of a single crazed ducking from around the corner. The monster's eyes were glossy and alien, with blood dripping like eye seeds into his lips. The crazed opened his mouth to reveal chomping teeth, sharpened as if he'd been gnawing upon bones.

Alayna stepped out and blasted the monster in the brain with a single bullet. Norah gasped, but the rest of them remained silent, watching as the monster collapsed to the ground. Ralph breathed heavily. The light of the morning no longer seemed so soft.

"Just a small bit of excitement this morning," Clay said, causing several of them to titter. He took a step to the side, making an arc around the dead body, in full sight of the Humvee. "They never let us down, do they? Always keep coming back for more. Like we're irresistible."

Clay stepped out onto Main Street and felt Alayna beside him. She placed a hand on his back as they moved toward the Humvee, easing her fingers over his tense muscles. Clay felt he could hear her encouragement in his head. “It’s going to be all right,” she seemed to say. “I’m right here. You’re not alone.”

But in that moment, Clay heard the sudden, rash scream of another crazed. He lurched around, realizing that as he’d been distracted, three monsters had marched up behind them, on the attack. Ralph lifted his gun even as a crazed wrapped his arms around his neck, trying to bite at his ear. Ralph blasted him once through the stomach, forcing the mutant back a few feet. But then he began to scramble forward, purple vomit and pus seeping from his stomach.

Daniels lifted his gun and shot the still-fighting crazed through the head, destroying him.

Clay felt they’d been caught off guard, lost and frightened, even before they’d had the time to get their bearings. As he lifted his gun, rushing past Alayna, one of the crazed latched himself onto Norah. Her eyes went wide and she screamed out, “JESUS. NO. PLEASE!”

But the mutant ripped his teeth into Norah’s throat, squirting blood all over Brandon’s shirt. Norah’s face went lax instantly. She folded to the ground, her long, flowered dress growing dirty on the pavement. Her eyelids flickered as the crazed monster began to gnaw at her skin, licking at her ear. And then, he took another massive bite at her cheek, her wrinkled skin clinging to his teeth.

“FUCK YOU!” Brandon cried, lifting a shocked and shaking hand to shoot a bullet through the crazed monster’s head. The mutant fell back instantly, like a toy, leaving just one more coming toward them.

Clay felt crazed himself, almost mad. He shot the last one, once a woman, who flung back, blood dripping from her ears. But Clay wasn't finished. He leaped forward, wrapping his hands around the monster's face and pummeled it into the pavement. Bits of bone spattered across Clay's chest and face, but he couldn't be finished—he couldn't be done that easy, not with all the destruction around. He was coated in blood up to his elbows, his eyes wide and panicked. He didn't realize where he was or what he was doing for several minutes more. And when he looked up, he was coated in grime. The crazed monster no longer had any semblance of being a person. Only bits of her clothing remained.

The troop stood in shocked silence, Norah splayed out before them, her neck and cheek bleeding ruby red onto the pavement. Her flowered dress was blotched and stained. Brandon knelt beside her, brushing his fingers through her silver hair. But Alayna continued to stare at Clay, at the animalistic way he hovered over that which he'd destroyed only moments before. She covered her mouth with her hand, shocked.

But Clay didn't have words for her. He didn't have words for any of them. His breath came jaggedly, in spurts. He leaned upon his knees, shuddering, and then rushed to the entrance of the candy store, where he began to vomit uncontrollably. He no longer had any feeling for his body's needs or wants.

Soon he was empty. He wiped himself clean and then turned toward the others, who were crying wordlessly over Norah's dead body. Brandon reached up and closed her eyelids. "She looks oddly peaceful. Like she didn't really want to go all the way, anyway. She was so tired," he whispered, his voice cracking. "She was so much more tired than she ever let on."

"And now she can rest," Alayna whispered. "But the rest of us. We should go." Her eyes snapped to Clay, as if to tell him to regain his composure. He was their leader. He needed to act like it.

Daniels and Brandon carried Norah to the side of the road, where they reasoned she'd lost too much blood to become a crazed monster. They covered her with a sheet, wishing they had time for a more fitting burial. And then they turned toward the waiting Humvee, its windshield reflecting the midmorning sunlight. Time was ticking, even when time didn't matter. They had to get moving.

Daniels slid into the driver's seat, indicating he thought Clay wasn't mentally strong enough to drive. Clay sat up front, the other four survivors behind them, their eyes lost and staring into the distance. Daniels revved the motor, and they began their necessary trek toward the outskirts of town. As they drove, nobody said a single word.

The energy field was flickering when they reached it, showing the suddenly bright blue sky on the outside. Daniels parked and tapped his fingers against the steering wheel. This was the only sound humming through their ears as they sat in sad contemplation.

"I pray to God we're doing the right thing," Jacobs said from the back seat, then. He gave voice to what everyone else was thinking. "I pray that we're not giving ourselves a death sentence by leaving the safety of the lab. We could have many more years there."

Clay shifted in his seat, clenching his fists. He felt enraged. "That would be no kind of life, Leland. No kind of life at all. We wouldn't have the love of our family members. I don't know your situation. But you must have had love once. You must know what it feels like, that richness of life. Without it, everything else feel empty. And we have to move forward. Together."

After Clay spoke, the team of six survivors sat in silence a moment longer, resolute in their decision to leave. On the other side of the flickering energy field, reality awaited them. Fear of the unknown clutched at their hearts. But with Clay as their leader, they had no choice but to proceed. He was right, after all. Remaining would mean no life at all.

ABOUT THE AUTHOR

Paul B Kohler is the Amazon Bestselling Author of Linear Shift author, as well as the highly-acclaimed novel, The Hunted Assassin. His remarkable novel series, The Borrowed Souls is also gaining traction with its readers. Aside from his longer works, a number of his short stories have been included in various anthologies. His latest short, Rememorations, has been included in The Immortality Chronicles - a Top 5 SF Anthology and Hot New Releases. Rememorations was also nominated for Best American Science Fiction.

When not practicing architecture, Paul works on his writing. He lives in Littleton, Colorado.

To learn more about him and his books, visit www.PaulKohler.net

Made in United States
North Haven, CT
12 February 2024

48684846R00176